D0681588

THE STILLEST DAY

THE STILLEST DAY

JOSEPHINE HART

THE OVERLOOK PRESS
WOODSTOCK & NEW YORK

First published in the United States in 1998 by
The Overlook Press, Peter Mayer Publishers, Inc.
Lewis Hollow Road
Woodstock, New York 12498

Library of Congress Cataloging-in-Publication Data

Hart, Josephine.
The stillest day / Josephine Hart.
p. cm.
I. Title
PR6058.A694845S75   1998   823'.414—dc21   98-16592
Manufactured in the United States of America

First Edition

1 3 5 7 9 8 6 4 2

ISBN 0-87951-894-4

FOR ADAM AND EDWARD

'What have I put into my pictures . . . ? I have put into them a small door opening on the mystery.'

Odilon Redon, 1888

THE STILLEST DAY

ONE

This is the history of the first year. It does not presage the last. I feel no guilt nor did I ever. And, though this surprises me, I had no pity.

Nothing in my past could have prepared me for what it is that I became. Nor for the moment when suddenly I was called upon to act and to bear witness to the very edge of my capabilities and almost beyond.

For nearly thirty years I lived a life of piety and duty. A life which rested upon the twin pillars of my vocation, art teacher, and my filial duty, that of loving daughter to my invalid widowed mother.

And so from the age of reason, which I believed to be seven, until my thirtieth year, I laid one foot before the other in a circular journey from home to school to home in my village world. One foot before the other quietly tapping out the years.

TWO

The geography of the place in which the essential nature of my soul was exposed is irrelevant. The exact position of that small village in county or country has no possible influence on my tale.

But we need a frame for the dream of life and this was mine. A village blessed with all that was necessary for village life: a church and churchyard, a school and a newly-built cottage hospital which within the community was a source of great pride.

This village, perhaps fearful, settled into the hills which surrounded it as though in search of sanctuary. It believed itself guarded by Grantleigh Manor which stood sentinel on the paramount hill, judiciously placed in a position more commanding even than that of the church. With its owner, Lord Grantleigh, landlord to many and most assuredly master of all he surveyed, this estate defined us and protected us.

A small factory, a foreshadowing of what was to come, crouched as death sometimes does in the furthermost corner of a painted landscape. The factory, barely discernible from the village, silently threatened us with a less amenable future: one which might distort the accepted pattern of our days and the ways which circumscribed our lives. Anxious, resistant to change, we endeavoured to ignore it and we most certainly distrusted it. Ours was historically a farming community and determined to remain so.

Sanctuary, it is believed, lies in small rural communities. Which is why those who fear the stranger will always choose the village, believing themselves safe amongst those they know. Yet the will to wound another has its source in passion: a passion which is ignited by inflammatory proximity to that which burns. This is an uncomfortable knowledge buried in a ritual of civic duty and familial bonds.

Many who flee villages fear being known. Few, only indeed the notorious, need ever flee the city. And if from its swaying aggregation of shadows the stranger bends with threatening intimacy, perhaps he has noted an implicit invitation.

I myself never sought the stranger and I was content for many years with familiar faces. The comfort of custom and the protection of prescribed procedure were essential to me. Within a rigid observance of habit, I believed I had created for myself a safe harbour. And though the city's blandishments of museums and theatres might perhaps have nourished me, its unceasing bedlam filled me with trepidation.

Also, my mother could not, indeed would not, move. She was fixed within her world. And within that small world she had created an even smaller one. A world constrained and contained, perhaps a preparation for burial. A burial made less cruel in prospect by the life-long knowledge of where, within the village graveyard, she would eventually lie. Since old departures and new arrivals are seen in their historical perspective, villages allow for the long contemplation of life and death.

Villages note and sometimes weep as family history repeats itself through the generations, creating tensions which shape entire families, tensions which are some-times resolved through patient revenge. And the admonitions of parents will always fail. In vain mothers of daughters point to the self-same dangers in village sons they once noted with enchantment in the fathers who came to court them. An old story told over and over again.

The time in which these events occurred was in the

time of my life. The great sweep of history in which so many unknown lives are drowned did not mark my days. I was blessed that neither war nor pestilence defaced my life nor my country. Thus for many years of my time on this earth I lived that most desired thing, a private life.

I have only sketched the time and place, the here and now, the then and there, of my life, for so little formed the final portrait of myself. A face, echoes, a sudden brutality. And the rest just slipped away.

My father used to say that life is a dream between two dreams, the dream of life and the dream of death. Our school had a plaque, donated by Lady Grantleigh, of an old English saying at which I often gazed:

> *Soone as we to bee beginne,*
> *Did beginne to bee undone.*

Do not look for your own reality in my story. Accept, if you will, my selection of what I regard as the most important events in my life. You might have chosen differently. But you are not Bethesda Barnet.

THREE

For many years my daily life followed the same pattern. Ritual sustained me in the belief that protection lay within its repetition. It is thus we are broken by habit. Its structure traps us. Laced in tight against vertiginous fall into chaotic truth, we cling terrified to the edifice, our fingers bleeding. Our entombed feet become numb in their hold. And we find when flight is essential that we cannot move. The structure which we thought protected us has left us paralysed.

Each morning I rose at six-thirty and bathed meticulously, monotonously, as though the water which flowed over my body obeyed the rhythm of the tides.

While my father lived, though he had never entered my bedroom after I attained a certain age, I felt it necessary to bathe while protecting my body with a robe which I placed on my shoulders after having removed my night-gown, always white, always cotton. Whenever it was stained, I secretly soaked the gown in cold water and salt in my room. I then wrapped it in towels to remove the dampness. When dry and innocent of blood, it joined other items which were taken to the house of a woman who, for reasons no one could remember, was called Ashes.

Ashes laundered for the village six days a week from morning till eight in the evening in the summer, six in the winter. In a large shed attached to the farm which her husband had left her as a parting gift – that and five children – Ashes bore down on the accumulated filth of our village with almost evangelical fervour.

She drubbed and thumped, pounded and punished each soiled and tainted item as though she rubbed out the sins which blackened our souls. Absolved and spotless again, for penance each item made its tortured way through an iron mangle. Then, as it hissed its steamy cries to Heaven, Ashes firmly pressed it into subjection, after which defeat it was returned to us each Thursday. And we believed we clothed ourselves in purity again.

I began my daily ablutions with the cleansing of my face and neck. These I did not scrub, being vain enough to wish to preserve the softness of my skin. I did not raise my arms for the robe would then have fallen from my shoulders, but stretched them in front of me and with long, slow movements rubbed the cloth up and down their length. I then bent down and, with my back still covered by my robe, washed my legs and thighs. Then allowing the robe to slide from one shoulder, I cleansed my body from shoulder blade down to the top of my thighs on my right side, repeating the same movement on my left side. Afterwards, I towelled myself dry. With fresh water I gently bathed my breasts and the lower regions of my body.

I never looked at my breasts but felt their mystery even as I touched them briefly. It seemed as if they waited with individual characteristics for some event in which they would play the central part. I felt a certain reverence, due to more than just the simple knowledge of their biological significance. I was not innocent of these matters, either anatomically or intellectually.

I dressed carefully in dark colours. My hair was worn neatly rolled in a bun on my neck and secured with pins. By these signs I recognised myself. And believed on reflection that I was Bethesda Barnet.

Each morning I approached my mother's room and stood outside breathing deeply for a few moments. Then, I tensed and forced myself into the rhythm of movements which would propel me towards her bed, where I would whisper,

"Mother, Mother dear."

As she turned to me, there always rose in me hatred and terror that the body can and does decay and that all the firmness and strength I had so lately bathed and dressed could come to this. Would come to this. If this residence of the soul which I had so lately tended could come to this, what journey would my soul undertake? And in what condition would the two continue on their path to the grave?

"The night was bad," she whispered, as she always did.

"Poor Mother," I replied, as I always did.

We then undertook a series of manoeuvres, painful for us both but essential for her difficult journey from bed to chair. Each morning, exhausted by our endeavours, she collapsed into its dark, garnet-coloured embrace.

Daily, I fetched a bowl of water and proceeded to wash her face and body in the same order as I had just washed my own. Wordlessly, I changed the water and handed her a clean cloth and averted my eyes as she tried to bathe the secret parts of her own body. A body which had once given birth to me and which once had suckled me. Afterwards, I helped to dress her. Then I brushed her hair and rolled and pinned it in such a way that she was simply the aged me. Thus attired for the day, silently and painfully we descended the stairs.

Slowly, as though to the music of a strange, disjointed minuet we took each step together, afraid of any slight misjudgement which might lead to a fatal fall. Hesitating at every step, as though caught in permanent descent, we presented to the eye a vision, a painting of two women, one young, the other old who once was as young as me.

FOUR

My mother's name was Margaret. She suffered from a progressive and extremely painful arthritis which, as the years continued, ensured an ever-increasing level of disability.

She had taught English in her own village school and knew much of Shakespeare by rote. Shakespeare was her passion. His characters were as real to her as anyone she knew in the village. She had a particular respect for Lear, detested Hamlet, and was most vehement in her defence of Othello, believing Desdemona a liar. When I was young she used these texts as moral tracts. *Lear*, naturally, brought her to the reiteration of the fifth commandment, "Honour thy father and thy mother".

She was not therefore, as you might have imagined, the desiccated mother of a spinster and the widow of a cautious school teacher. There was a time in my childhood when she had been subject to terrors which seemed to explode with a shocking ferocity and then to dissipate in a climactic burst of laughter. But that was long ago and, for many years now, her body had trapped her and her mind had succumbed.

My father's name was Alexander. A name which, though he bore it manfully, he had always regarded as an embarrassment. The name Alexander was more suited to one of a different stratum of society. As a teacher he had been habitually referred to as "Mr Barnet". And even his close friends deferred to him. They felt that to laugh and joke with Alexander in front of their children would have undermined his authority. So "Mr Barnet" he remained, until he died in the last months of my teacher training.

On my father's death, the school council, under the final authority of Lord Grantleigh, decided that my mother and I could remain in our house. I would of course have been entitled to accommodation in a small, single teacher's residence attached to the school and close to that of the headmaster. However, my mother's illness combined with my father's many years of dedicated service to the school, decided the matter in my favour.

Was it my good fortune, therefore, that my mother was an invalid? Life metes out strange justice and the distress of others, even their death, can contribute to one's own life certain rewards.

And so, within that small house in which we were allowed to remain, we adhered to a rigid pattern of time. We put down each day carefully, as though it were linen already pressed, which fell back into its folds and was carefully returned to its proper place.

At seven-thirty, we breakfasted on bread, milk and cheese. I then laid out, on a table close to the large winged-chair in which my mother spent much of her day, a glass, a jug of water and her favourite books, the Bible, a copy of *Paradise Lost* and whichever Shakespeare play she was rereading.

Afterwards, a short time was spent on the organisation and cleaning of my small household. Strength made me mistress here. At eight-thirty I walked the same path each day to school. As I was protected from time-consuming gossip by a reputation for reticence, at no later than four o'clock I returned home. Before I retired to my room to paint, I sometimes read aloud to my mother, a favourite poem or a scene from Shakespeare. A habit which began in childhood and which pleased us both to continue.

Supper at six-thirty was fish or meat simply cooked accompanied by some vegetables. After supper if the weather allowed we took a slow walk through the village to the church. And perhaps, as we moved together on our well-worn path, we presented to the world a veritable vision of virtue.

Often when we returned, a young man whose name was Samuel and who, it was assumed by all, wished for my hand in marriage, came to call. He was, I suppose, that recognisable symbol, the suitable suitor. One whose gaze is always open and yet, when one looks more closely, is perceived to be strangely opaque.

Within that morning-till-evening fortress of habit lay another immutable structure, one built on acquiescence to the reverberation of bells. A tonal world in which our thoughts shuffled methodically and obediently from one subject to another; a dreamy delirium of convocation.

A subtle acknowledgement of privilege dictated a daily monotony of movement through the school. The reverential and deferential demeanour of the teaching staff as those in authority glided past, was abruptly transformed in the practice of their own power. Even a slight inclination of the head or an extension of an arm had the force of a command. And pupils were quickly marshalled into the precision of place which marks the *corps de ballet* or the regiment at arms.

Each morning, I took up my position second left of

the headmaster, Mr Slope, and listened in silence as he intoned the prayers for assembly. After assembly, each teacher moved to his or her allocated position in the building. Clockwork figures well rehearsed in an ancient choreography.

And if we seemed to move through the school with heads held at a certain angle of reverence, perhaps it was because Christian architecture is a very pointed thing. Resembling as they did hands joined in adoration, the windows and doors in our school guided our eyes and thoughts towards Heaven.

Though the headmaster's house possessed Norman aspects, the school building followed the principles of Augustus Welby Northmore Pugin, with whose ideas on architecture Lord Grantleigh, patron of our school, as he was of everything else, professed himself in agreement.

As always, Lord Grantleigh seemed to mock his own pronouncements. I had often noted and admired this tendency in him. I thought it showed great cleverness in ensuring that no one believed him too passionate and therefore vulnerable on any issue.

"It is fitting that a school should follow Mr Pugin's principles. After all, Miss Barnet, we prepare our young people for lives of propriety, do we not?"

"Yes, Lord Grantleigh."

THE STILLEST DAY

"Then perhaps you will paint the school for me, Miss Barnet? As it is. Cruel, I know, to demand only reproduction from the artist. However, I would ask you to take great care to avoid your own propensity towards classicism, which they tell me is now regarded as a form of paganism. These are perilous times . . . times of antinomy."

"Antinomy, Lord Grantleigh?"

"Between classical and romantic. Between Christianity and paganism. But then, so much was lost in the journey between paganism and Christianity. Would you not agree, Miss Barnet? And for such an uncertain gain. However, Mr Pugin seems so certain and certainty must be admired."

"Oh, I'm certain of that, Lord Grantleigh."

I sometimes recall this conversation when I look upon the architecture of my current abode. And smile. And feel I have the right to do so.

FIVE

As art teacher, I was favoured with a small room in which the desire for light had justified a certain sacrifice of proportion. Though much engaged by light and its capture, I believed there were also many shades of dark. And that the dark was often underrated by painters.

The allocation of this much coveted space was within the gift of Lord Grantleigh.

"Miss Barnet is an artist and into her days at school must flow as much light as is possible. Would you not agree, Mr Slope?"

"I would indeed, Lord Grantleigh."

It was a habit of our headmaster, Mr Slope, to agree with everything Lord Grantleigh said. Thus there existed between them a most commodious relationship.

The light in my room flowed through high windows whose glass arched towards God in a febrile act of adoration. These windows seemed virtually trapped between curved oak panels. A painted dark-blue roundel depicting The Annunciation was centred between each window. It was perhaps a reminder that life is a gift direct from God and, in this case, "had arrived independently of man", as Lord Grantleigh once remarked. And, as the roundel drew the eye further towards Heaven, it must be assumed that the deep blue of the sky had been chosen to emphasise the trajectory.

Thus our pupils did not lack guidance towards Christianity in the architectural structure of their school. And the asymmetrical nature of the building gave each classroom an individual ambience and each teacher a deeply proprietorial feeling for his or her room. Young children in their first year at school sometimes felt themselves to be lost in an illogical labyrinth and realised that they would have to work hard to find their way. A perfect training for life, particularly the spiritual life.

In this light-filled room to which I daily made my way, followed by my young pupils, I concentrated initially on the rules of drawing. Though this delayed their discovery of the joy of painting and composition, I felt certain the discipline would allow them greater freedom of expression later. Thus I was taught and thus I taught. As a good teacher should.

Occasionally, carefully selected paintings taken from a book donated to the school by the Lord Grantleigh were discussed in class. I taught children from age seven to fourteen, after which they left me, either to become pupils at the school in the nearby town or to help on their parents' farms or to work in the local factory.

Before they left, I taught them what I believed was essential to them. Which was much, much less than I knew. I fulfilled, therefore, the great responsibility of the adult. I told the essential lies. And left the rest in obscurity. As was my duty.

Though I always reacted with suitable modesty to Lord Grantleigh's statements concerning my abilities — which he frequently made to the Bishop and any visiting dignitaries — I knew myself to be an artist.

Lord Grantleigh's admiration of my work, paintings of the school and church, mundane though it was in subject matter if not in execution, led to our regular Thursday afternoon meetings in the conservatory of Grantleigh Manor. And thus, over time, after each of his visits to his mother who now lived in Paris, I was introduced to certain concepts which seeped into my consciousness, a subtle colour-wash of an uncertain hue.

Croquis, he explained, was the sudden drenching of the artistic mind by the first vision which must be rendered immediately in a few strokes. And then he quoted Delacroix, an artist of whom I had not heard. "If you are not skilful enough to sketch a man falling out of a window during the time it takes him to fall from the fifth storey to the ground, you will never be able to produce monumental work."

Had Delacroix, I wondered, been at all interested in the aftermath of the fall with its commingling of the personal and biblical?

Etude, Lord Grantleigh continued, was the obsessively detailed rendering of individual aspects of the human body or landscape; an exquisite narrowing down from that first vision to minute investigation. This was also ecstatically described.

Ebauche, the underpainting. Lord Grantleigh listed the typical palette as though he were singing a well-known hymn; silver-white, Naples yellow, yellow ochre, ochre de ru, red ochre, cinnabar, ivory or cork black, and Prussian blue. Almost mathematically he explained the arrangement of the palette for the *ébauche* into three divisions: one for the light areas, another for the shadows, and the last for the *demi-teintes*. His new-found passion was for *les demi-teintes*, believing, as he did, in a gradation of light as it moved to dark, as though he were wholly innocent of the possibility of an immediate transition.

And thus, in an area in which I believed myself to be the master, the sudden re-arrangement of old concepts and the introduction of a new philosophy subtly changed my perception.

During that summer, I sometimes thought as I walked back from Grantleigh Manor how *croquis*, *étude*, *ébauche*, each a stage in preparation for a final painting, formed an emblematic pattern which could be applied to life. I absorbed it all and disagreed with much. "Colour versus line," Lord Grantleigh said, was the painterly debate of our time. However, I believed they pressed upon each other. Line contained and restrained the colour which would otherwise escape, and, as such, I believed it was master of the scene.

The lines of my life were, as I now discern, classical. There was a time when I believed them to be romantic.

SIX

Though I had known Samuel Keans all my life it was only in the past five years we had started walking out together. Samuel was not in any great hurry to marry. His father's farm demanded all his attention and a wife needed to be more than just a comfort on a farm. I was ill-suited to such a life. A fact of which I felt sure his father had made him aware.

However, as is often the case, my unsuitability in his father's eyes, while not to be ignored, also ignited something in him. Perhaps Samuel felt a certain manliness in reassuring me. Nevertheless, it was a very controlled courtship.

When Samuel spoke to me he often spoke of love. It was, one was led to believe, a precondition of marriage that the emotion must be at least referred to during the time, be it months, or in my case years, before the event.

On summer evenings, the three of us sat in our tiny garden, my mother, Samuel and I, and talked of village matters and of his farm. And my mother always sat between us so that we presented, whether in public or in private, a most proper picture.

When I walked with him to the end of the village and back again, we observed certain rules of distance, as though each of us had a perfect understanding of an almost algebraic formula of the acceptable propinquity of the unmarried. We walked through the village past windows through which we were discreetly noted on our prescribed journey. And the watchers waited. For surely a decision must soon be made.

Perhaps because of the delay, over time I began to lose faith in this ritual courtship. Perhaps, I even told myself, it mattered little. Marriage followed by the birth of a son or daughter was an old pattern. One which consumed the years. Care for children followed by years of care by them: another ancient rhythm to which like everyone else I must in time succumb.

The step towards marriage with me was a difficult one for Samuel and may have been the reason why our physical conjunctions were so restrained. Hands were held, mouths kissed, body pressed to body for only that period of time which would not shame either of us by the movement and swellings and pressures that are the precursor of a more complete act. An act which can never be revoked and after which all is changed.

However, this long drawn-out courtship was still precious to me. I was not a spinster without hope but a woman with some prospect of marriage.

My mother's questions still echo in my mind.

"Bethesda. Bethesda, can you hear me?"

My mother and I spoke rarely and always guardedly on the subject of my possible marriage.

"Yes, Mother."

"Does Samuel never speak of marriage?"

"No, Mother."

"After all this time?"

"Even after all this time. And Mother, it is less than six months since you and I last spoke of this."

"Do I intrude?"

"No, Mother."

"Your father might have found a way to talk to him . . ."

"Man and man alike?"

"Yes. I married your father when I was twenty-four."

"I know, Mother. And you had me when you were thirty."

"A long wait. A long fear. For us both. Your father wanted children but I could only have you."

"Only child, only me."

"He was very pleased by you."

"I know, Mother. You always tell me."

"He was not a talkative man. He was so proud that you wanted to teach."

"I know. Though I don't understand why. It was an obvious decision for me. All my life I listened to him; '*Educo* to draw out. Not *Induco* to force in.' It seemed a fine philosophy. Though I find little that I consider original in those I teach and very little to bring out."

"I thought you loved your teaching."

"Love it? No, I do not think so. But I am content."

She smiled. And her smile conveyed to me her belief that such contentment was meagre indeed.

SEVEN

Master Orpington, my next-door neighbour, teacher of English for over thirty years, died suddenly on a Sunday morning. He was on his way to church. As he walked up the steep hill which he mounted so often, for he was a deeply religious man, he silently collapsed before the summit.

The congregation fluttered around the dying man. And they blotted out for him a last view of sky. The final vision of his life was of a ring of terrified faces drawing closer and closer together until light was obliterated.

Later, the villagers comforted Mrs Orpington with the fact that her husband's last journey on this earth had been one towards God. A journey which they were certain had been continued by his soul. Mrs Orpington seemed soothed by this thought. She left the village shortly afterwards to live with Clare, the only child the marriage had produced. No doubt, she became a help domestically to her daughter and son-in-law who, perhaps in rebellion, had produced three boys in five years. Though one can only guess at these matters, I thought it possible the mother, grandmother to the three boys, would blight the couple's marriage.

For I had a dream of the union between man and woman that would barely allow for children. And one which would never allow a parent to enter whatever set of rooms in which I acted out my dream.

Where did it come from, my dream of that strange dance, the steps of which seemed to mesmerise certain men and women? Behind them laboured the rest, weary dancers always slightly out of step, always angry with what they heard as too slow a beat to the music or breathless at what they interpreted as a sudden arpeggio; exhausting themselves in a fruitless search for what is in fact a sudden undeserved invitation to the death of self. Had paintings, novels or poetry shaped these chimerical longings? Or had I simply dreamed them? And found in that dream the very essence of myself?

Master Orpington had not been a dreamer. Through the shared wall between our two houses drifted the sounds of distant angers and occasional scuffles, from which I gleaned the essential nature of their marriage.

While he and Mrs Orpington had lived in that small

house to which he would never return, they themselves had seemed to me like heavy pieces of furniture placed in position at the beginning of the occupation, never to be moved.

From these fixed positions they had guided their daughter Clare, until she made her own rather wild departure from them to her husband. He was a loud and heavy man who almost broke the furniture of the house and the structure of the Orpington marriage. For a while it seemed possible that violence would erupt. However, a wedding planned and executed with speed soothed everyone.

Daughters, my mother often said, shame a family in a particular way and leave it naked before the world. A warning to me, perhaps. For my mother and I both knew that a family shamed in a village is shamed for generations. And in repetition the history of an old sin achieves an almost biblical resonance.

Here in this known place I learned from the lives of others. As they no doubt learned from mine. And mine is a lesson which will be long taught.

EIGHT

His rain-washed face was what I first saw. It was turned to the heavens which drenched the wetness further, so that rivulets of water ran down his white skin. And in that instant I longed to let my hair loose to dry the unknown wonder of that vision.

I leaned against my front door and trapped my hands behind me lest they unfurl the cloth of my hair and I would be destroyed.

He gently pushed the front door to his new home, which seemed almost reluctant to give way to him. Finally, it opened and he disappeared into Master Orpington's old house. It had lain empty, sleeping side by side with mine, since Mrs Orpington's departure.

He was the new teacher who had come to replace Master Orpington. He had arrived early. No doubt, to make preparations for his wife. I knew his marital status from the headmaster's announcement. All this I knew.

THE STILLEST DAY

So I knew everything. The other, was. And he was the other. And I knew that this was all there was to know.

I slid silently back into my house. And in the hall I stared into the long mirror which captured me, wet and white, and the vision of him was on my face. This tracery of his face on mine was so clear that his and mine seemed to form a single portrait.

I knew the mystery of mirrors. I knew the pirouette of the eye which makes us recognise ourselves, falsely. The reversed image of truth is impossible for our human eye to look upon. And so we mould our vision to our spiritual capabilities and, of necessity, believe yet another essential lie.

Suddenly, my face felt as though it was being stripped of his and was about to become naked again. The translucent mask of his face on mine was being sucked by greedy particles of light into the heart of the mirror.

In desperation I pressed my face onto the hard reflection of cold glass until breath was almost impossible. Still I could not catch him. All of him was fading from me. I covered my face with my hands in a fierce attempt to force the outline of his face into my very skin. Still he eluded me. I fell against the wall in terror.

Now I had only memory. The memory of a vision which I wished to trap and gaze upon forever. I felt

impelled to act immediately and ran to the stairs. To my
mother's old cry:

"Bethesda, is that you. . . ?"

I called my old reply:

"Yes. Yes, it's me, Mother."

I almost fell into my room, such was my fear that I
might lose the glory of that image. I closed my eyes and
tried frantically to capture my memory of the rain on his
face. To recall the liquid veil that covered and uncovered
him. Could I capture in what was constantly flowing a
reflection for a second of myself?

Hanging on the walls of my room I had a collection
of mirrors which my grandmother had given me. I
selected a small, oval mirror with a mother-of-pearl
surround. And on to it, slowly and carefully, I painted
his face.

I painted it as I had first seen it. I painted it as though
it was a face which, disembodied, floated onto the water
of the mirror to capture my own face on his. And to
capture his face as when, moments ago, its contours had
traced themselves on mine, as I gazed and gazed,
reflected and refracted, skin and hair and bones of two,
shimmering into one. And my own face was suddenly a
unique thing because it was reflected in this other. This

only other. And we merged together in the reality of the dreams we dream in mirrors.

To my first vision his face was wet, in order that I could drink from it. It was white and silver, so I would never again be in darkness. Should I long for rest, his hair would hide me in a kind of velvet, black blindness, momentarily and immediately. Then rested, I could turn again to the subtle silver beauty of his face. To my first vision, he was light and dark. And in his face I would find life's rhythm of night and day.

My father's mother had given me two shawls — one heavy with silver, the other with gold threading, a treasured gift, her legacy to me. I wore them rarely, only on special evenings; the two parties at Grantleigh Manor which annually celebrated the New Year and the Summer Solstice.

I took the oval mirror on which I had painted his face and carefully wrapped it in the silver-threaded shawl. I felt silver best reflected his whiteness. I laid his mirrored face in the last drawer of my day bureau, a Jacobean piece from my grandmother's home, for I wished him to be safe. I did not live alone. Though it was years since my mother had undertaken the short journey from her bedroom to mine, invalids can surprise with their sudden strength.

Trembling, I stood in my room which I now shared with another. I knew everything should change. I knew that my behaviour in the days to come must of necessity be more delicate. No untoward view of me must defile his vision.

I would not unpin my hair nor arrange my dress before his image, nor let him know that my choice might have been dictated by his eyes — those eyes which might from their mirrored darkness pierce for a moment the obdurate wood of the bureau. Since he was to live with me here in my room, I would not dishonour him. I would not betray myself or him. And thus I would never lose him.

Then another dread consumed me. Was there something in his eyes I dared not look upon? Or in mine when I gazed through his eyes back into my own? Perhaps I might not ever have the courage to look upon his face again? Perhaps his silver-cauled face must be entombed forever in the wooden vault of my bureau.

I had looked upon a face. A single vision had revealed to me my life's destiny. A natural worshipper, I had found my God.

That is the history of my first vision of him. And, like the history of the first year, it did not presage the last.

NINE

From then on, my body and my soul seemed to separate, my soul to go about its secret worship, my body, a lonely entity, left to thread its well-worn path through the known hours of my known days. That body which once I had believed to be the adequate even fine residence of a mind at peace with the internal and external contours of my daily life.

The controlled actions of those days, with their endlessly repeated rhythm which I once thought would shelter me forever, were now undertaken with Coppelia-like movements.

And in my home I began to sense that some vital energy rested in the excessive closeness of one house to the other, as they lay side by side in almost miasmic proximity. And the shared wall which supported identical structures became in my mind dangerously fluid.

I knew the proportions, spherical, cubic, volumetric,

of every room in which he walked. And this profound familiarity made it possible for me to imagine myself an ethereal presence which followed him wherever he went.

I could follow him to the uttermost parts of his domain everywhere, everywhither. Past the narrow, heavy door which opened onto steep steps down into an equally narrow hallway. And into one or other of the rooms whose symmetry of proportion demonstrated a futile yearning for equilibrium in all things.

Therefore, in his home, where he believed himself to be most protected from a stranger's gaze, from my mind's eye he had no escape.

As I strained to hear what had never been spoken, real conversations became like distant echoes. The voices of my mother, Lord Grantleigh and Samuel Keans seemed as though they floated in a gentle reverberation. I engaged with the world in a monotone of mesmerism. My real self was whispered to me in reflected images.

And from then on, I seemed to move forward as though hypnotised towards the stillest day. As though I heard its secret, terrible music from far away.

TEN

I remember her arrival. She was small and she was pregnant. And because she was small she carried her pregnancy inelegantly. She glanced at me, for I was leaving my house at the time; and, with a little smile and perhaps too shy to speak, she entered her new home. The house which had once belonged to Master Orpington: the house which was the very mirror-image of my own.

Master Orpington's ghost would now move amongst strangers. And the house which had noted his death would shortly witness a birth. Poor passive houses, always acted upon. Perhaps they have their favourite inhabitants. But, like well-trained servants, houses must perform the same duty of care to all with practised grace.

She was followed by a young man carrying a heavy, oak chest. Though he was tall and broad, he had a noticeably rounded, almost female, face. Was he disturbed, I wondered, by the femininity of the features which made him so resemble his sister? He was a strong young man and did not seem to strain under the weight of the bureau. Then he carried another chest across the threshold and the dressing of the house to the taste of its new inhabitants had begun.

It was the custom in the village to bring gifts of welcome to newcomers. My mother and I waited a day or two, lest eagerness be misinterpreted as intrusion. We agreed that Wednesday, this being Monday, would be the correct day for such a visit.

After a short discussion, my mother and I decided on the gift of Christmas roses from our garden. Thus armed, we proceeded slowly, she leaning on my arm as always, with a predatory grasp. It was disturbingly easy to forget the family of three, Mr and Mrs Orpington and their daughter Clare, who had lived beside me all my life.

Even minor arrivals and departures have an old rhythm. I gently raised the iron knocker in the shape of a lion's head, which had enthralled me as a child, and with as little sound as possible I made our presence known.

"I am Bethesda Barnet and this is my mother, Mrs

Margaret Barnet." I held the roses towards her. "We both hope you will be happy with us here in the village."

"Oh, I'm sure we will." She had merry eyes and a light voice. "My name is Mary Pearson. Do come in."

Falteringly, my mother manoeuvred her way down into their hallway, preceded by our hostess whose heaviness and slowness had a different source. As we entered their sitting room, I noted again how closely this room resembled our own. Indeed, little more than a predominance of the colour pink and the addition of an unusually large settle differentiated them.

As we sipped our tea, there was an initial, awkward silence. Neither my mother nor I asked the date of the expected birth, it being too delicate a matter to pursue. My mother had gleaned from someone in the village that the date of their wedding would not normally have indicated so advanced a state of pregnancy. My mother had earlier intimated to me that the state of pregnancy might have preceded the marriage and might indeed have determined it.

Her remark lacked charity. My mother's pain was always alleviated by the contemplation of others' distress. Her suffering allowed her to absolve herself of certain moral imperatives. Since I knew her well, I knew she would have found charity the easiest to relinquish. She was her Faith. Hope had become a habit. Charity was a virtue which had never come naturally to her.

With Mary Pearson we spoke of the school and of her husband's passion for his subject, English. We spoke of his great love of poetry, of which evidently he could, like my mother, quote many, many lines – indeed entire scenes from Shakespeare and much of *Paradise Lost*. I spoke a little of my love of art. She interrupted with the knowledge, which pleased me, that her husband had heard my painting was most highly regarded.

Solicitous of my mother, Mary Pearson swooped towards her with little cakes which she had baked herself; and an hour and a half had passed before we left.

The merry eyes of Mary Pearson did not seem especially to glow or darken as she spoke of her husband. Her voice seemed to light upon his name gently. As though within its cadence no false note had ever been struck.

ELEVEN

His first visit to my house I remember thus.

"And when is your due date, my dear Mary?"

My mother and Mary Pearson had now become more intimate. Perhaps they were united by motherhood. One had traversed its cruel but wondrous state and the other was about to embark upon it. And Mary Pearson now had no choice in the matter. What was within must move out or be wrenched from her, perhaps unwilling to leave but also without choice in the matter. To me, motherhood was a mysterious land almost unbearable in its contours: a land from which many returned with strange and terrible stories.

"March, I believe, Mrs Barnet."

"They say that being so . . . large means it will be a boy."

"I've heard that too, Mrs Barnet."

"And Mr Pearson? Does he long for a son?"

"Perhaps. Though he has never expressed a preference. He will collect me later. Do tell him that you think it will be a boy."

This conversation took place as I prepared some tea for my mother and for her round and twinkling guest. I had returned early from my classes to consider a special lesson for the next day. I laid the tea before them. Then I turned and walked serenely to the door. I responded to a certain knowledge that now at this exact moment he stood outside my house. Even as he raised the knocker I opened the door to him and spoke softly,

"Mr Pearson."

His hand fell to his side. I saw that it was a long hand with nails cut straight across. And that the thumb turned a little backwards.

"Miss Barnet. Good evening. My wife is here, I believe."

"Yes, Mr Pearson."

He followed me down the short hall towards them, a man amongst women, one of whom carried his child. Refusing tea, he placed his hand upon his wife's shoulder and I found that I could study it again. Ink marks, naturally, on the fingertips. Was that a scar I glimpsed on the palm when his hand moved from her shoulder to her elbow to support her as she struggled to rise from the chair?

"Mrs Barnet, it is so kind of you to entertain Mary."

"On the contrary, it is kind of her to visit me. I walk with difficulty now and therefore receive visitors with great pleasure. You must be eager for the birth of your child. I really believe, Mr Pearson, you will have a son."

"And why is that, Mrs Barnet?"

"Because, as I explained to dear Mary, she is . . . large for her time."

He did not react at all. He simply smiled and said:

"I am not an expert in these matters."

"Nor am I," said Mary quickly, and together they left. Man and pregnant wife. And we remained, mother and daughter. Each a couple, each alone in small, identical houses. Houses which almost encroached upon each other. And in one house a couple, male and female, lay side by side.

After their departure, I spoke some pleasantries about the ideal couple. Then I slipped into my room to begin my work. The image of his hand was transferred by me, after an outline drawing, onto a small, silver hand-mirror. It had long lain innocently on top of my bureau and was part of a set with brush and comb — my parents' gift to me on gaining my majority.

I painted the beauty of his palm, outstretched to denote acceptance, in the lower right-hand corner of the mirror. It was the right hand and I believed that I did it justice.

As I worked, I thought that the face, hands and occasionally the arms are all that women normally see of the body of an unknown man. Of the unknown bodies of women, men see more. Arms stretched naked from a sleeve of silk, or cotton on summer nights. Throat and shoulders decorously exposed on chaperoned evenings at ritual village gatherings. It is an old arrangement of sanctioned allure.

While I worked, his hand moved over my face in the mirror. When I had finished, I held the mirror above my head and looked into it. And it seemed to me that his hand stroked my hair and eyes. And I approved its movements.

TWELVE

The Lord Grantleigh
invites
Mrs Margaret Barnet and Miss Bethesda Barnet
to Grantleigh Manor
for
The New Year's Ball

Though Samuel hated to dance, he accompanied my mother and me through the long tapestry-hung hall of the Manor into the drawing room. This room was annually transformed by Lord Grantleigh for the New Year party. It now blushed an English-skin pink, unsinful, or perhaps redolent of an assumed innocence. And, as the room had subtly changed its hue, perhaps in response so did we.

On either side of an Elizabethan chimney-piece hung

four pale-rose panels. Each was decorated with roundels
and cartouches. With picturesque scenes of pastoral
settings within surrounds of foliate scrolls, cherubs and
cornucopia, they created the atmosphere of a sun-
drenched late-autumn garden. On the opposite side of
the ballroom, heavy velvet curtains the colour of dull
gold, on which multi-coloured birds had been painted,
fell from ceiling to floor. And in this walled world of
velvet and painted panels, internal and external parame-
ters seemed to fall away. We moved through the room
as though dreaming, in a delicious confusion of rosy
warmth.

My mother joined the women who watched the
women who waited to be invited to the dance. Samuel
guided me onto the floor and awkwardly led me in the
steps nature had not deigned we should dance together.

Then, as we turned, a sudden imprint on my mind of
Mathew Pearson's face. Glimpsed fleetingly and as
quickly lost in the constant drift and swell of faces at the
far end of the ballroom. Again, suddenly, a vision of his
body and that of his wife moving to music. And I
watched as with difficulty he stretched the length of his
arm around the great protuberance of his wife's
pregnancy. I saw him move too slowly to the rise and
fall the music dictated. Mary Pearson wore a dress in a

becoming shade of blue. Elegance being impossible in her condition, she had wisely chosen adornment by colour.

I wore white. I had allowed myself a more elaborate arrangement of my hair than was my habit. It was held in place by old lapis lazuli pins which I had bought as a gift to myself on the day I received my Teacher's Certificate. We bowed to each other, Mathew and Mary Pearson, the married and fertile couple; and Samuel Keans and Bethesda Barnet, a man and woman in an unmarried, unconsummated union.

When the selection had ended, Samuel and I made our way towards my mother. Within minutes, we were joined by Mathew and Mary Pearson. My mother patted a cushion of a dark and sullen green and Mary Pearson placed herself awkwardly upon it. Her voluminous blue dress obliterated its unwelcoming hue. I stood between the two men and we formed a trinity arranged, perhaps, in adoration of motherhood past and future.

"The waltz wasn't designed for these months, I have to confess, Miss Barnet." Mary Pearson spoke, panting a little.

Why does she persist in calling me Miss Barnet?

". . . I mean, Bethesda. Mathew always refers to you as Miss Barnet, so I follow suit . . ."

"You're always graceful, my dear."

"Why thank you, Mrs Barnet."

My mother seemed entranced by Mary Pearson. Motherhood, maybe? Is it possible that all mothers desire to share this state with others? Or was it simply that Mary Pearson was more to my mother's liking? "Only daughter" does not denote favourite and never can.

"Mathew. Don't you think. . . ?"

Mary Pearson looked at me, then back at her husband.

"Miss Barnet, may I. . . ?"

Mathew Pearson asked me if I wished to dance with him. At which point Samuel quickly sat down beside my mother as though grateful to be relieved of the responsibility of once more leading me onto the floor.

In sanctioned proximity I stood before a slender man. And there was little to separate his body and mine. As I moved closer to him, it seemed to me that his shoulders formed a straight line, like that of The Cross. My palm, as I laid it in accepted benediction, detected a slight protrusion of bone along the scapula. A minor defect in the structure.

My eyes, which I did not raise, rested naturally on his neck. I was reminded of the story of the woman desecrated by the doctor who had come to her aid after she had attempted the sin of suicide. Her bleeding neck aroused in him such lust that he destroyed himself. My mother, in whose village this tragedy had occurred, always followed the telling of the tale with a sigh, "Ah, poor man". An uncommon charity of soul for her. These were the thoughts on which my mind rested, as my eyes rested on the neck of Mathew Pearson.

"Miss Barnet?"

"Yes, Mr Pearson?"

"I feel somewhat embarrassed. I fear my wife may have forced this dance upon you. Naturally you would have preferred to dance with Mr Keans. I am sorry."

Still my eyes did not leave his neck.

"Mr Pearson, in accepting your invitation to dance I did in fact please myself."

"I'm relieved to hear that. Perhaps then, Miss Barnet, you might look at me for a moment. Mary is looking at us and her expression seems to imply that I may have offended you."

"You must know your wife's expressions well to detect so much from a distance."

"We have known each other since childhood."

"So you watched her face grow?"

"What a strange way of putting it. But yes, I watched her face grow."

"Why hers . . . so watched?"

"Sadly, my only sister died when she was eight. Mary's family came to the village the same year. Mary's age and appearance, though not identical, were similar. She soothed my mother in some way."

"She has a way with mothers."

"Yes, she is most womanly and never more so than now."

"It must please your mother greatly that you and Mary married."

"Yes. Mary and I were much encouraged by my mother."

"And your father. . . ?"

"My father rarely commented on such matters."

The music stopped. The dance ended. The end of the dance shocks us, although we know it must always end. I removed my hand from his shoulder and the slight protrusion of bone which I had felt as we danced seemed now to be lightly etched on my palm. And the perfectly recalled vision of his neck seemed to lie like softest silk upon my cheek. A feeling on my skin of an imaginary imprint of his neck and shoulder-bone slipped upon me, a web-like shawl.

Mathew Pearson escorted me back to our respective watchers. They smiled as we approached. My mother sat beside Samuel, my official partner to the dance, a man intended for other privileges in my life. And on her other side sat Mathew Pearson's wife, Mary, waiting for motherhood and for him.

That is the history of how I first touched him.

THIRTEEN

The first step back from reality is rarely the last. The seduction of the imagination beckons to us from the shadowy corridors of the mind.

Touch now joined with vision to create a dreaming landscape. A mirage with sudden outlines of meticulous detail. The exact whiteness of skin. A geometry of bony extrusion. And so that first touch, like the first vision, drew me deeper into dreams.

For the pressure of his hand on my back, however light, had forced the blood to slow, almost to stop, and then resume its movement through my veins. Differently. He had touched me. He had changed the very flow of my life.

It was as though that fleeting physical conjunction on the dance floor had evinced transmission of some strange organism which now circulated within me. And, like a narcotic, it further separated my dreaming soul from the familiar truths of my daily life.

Some sweet apathy descended on me. And I wandered through the contours of my structured days as though some metaphysical vacancy had consumed them.

FOURTEEN

But even in dreams the point of satiation always slips further away from us. I now hungered for a larger surface on which to reproduce the lines of his shoulders in their exact dimensions.

The hall mirror which had first reflected the tracery of his face on mine was perfect in both its proportion and its symbolism. However, its disappearance would be noted by my mother. What was needed was a reason for its removal. I was an intelligent woman. The solution to this problem was therefore not beyond my intellect. Nor as I began to realise was it beyond my curious, late-unveiled cunning.

This contemplation of deception caused me no guilt. Through the years and without complaint I had carried in my soul the increasingly heavy cross of my mother. Who was the woman who helped carry The Cross? I do not recall her name. But I, Bethesda, had carried my cross. And for many years I had also bent my back in order to alleviate my mother's pain, as was my duty. I was strong. I could therefore carry the mirror to my room.

The next morning I spoke to my mother:

"I did not want you to see the broken glass, Mother, knowing only too well how superstitious you are."

Then, with a slight smile:

"It happened in the night as you slept. I mean to replace the mirror with a painting whose dimensions will exactly match its outline on the wall."

"You are so gifted, Bethesda."

"The painting will be for you, Mother."

"Bethesda, you should paint only for yourself. You do enough for others."

"I shall choose then, Mother. And hope to please you."

Another mirror with similar dimensions could in time have been acquired. We were not poor, but had few funds for decoration.

Though my arm and palm had rested on the front of Mathew Pearson's shoulder I wanted to reproduce the image of The Cross which had first come to me while we danced.

I had placed the mirror inside my wardrobe. It lay

along the back panel behind my clothes. Their darkness had always seemed to me correct, and each time I opened my wardrobe my white silk evening gown was like a shaft of moonlight in the blackness. I laid it, bridal-like, upon my bed. Then I slid my dark, lifeless clothes to one side and secured them with ribbon so that they resembled a single, multi-skirted garment waisted in pale green satin. I fell to my knees and in the faint light which filtered from a side window I painted in earth-red a dark-timbered cross beam, one which seemed to cry out for the iconic head and arms which it has always embraced. But I resisted. I painted Mathew Pearson's shoulders, suited, in that moment of dark blue when it slips into black.

My own reflection broken by the lines of blue-black and earth-red seemed like that of the succubus, silent and predatory. And I felt that I was both absorber and absorbed. I covered my face to break the vision and moved to the centre of my room.

And I realised that I now had a collection of mirror-paintings which included his face, his palm and his shoulders. A series of exquisitely wrought *études*.

That night before I slept, I rested on these parts of him and they absorbed my own reflection. And the cold purity of our intermingling glinted and gleamed through the night. So that either in dreams or reality he was with me upon the pillow, shining slightly in the mirrored darkness.

Later, when I lay exhausted on my bed, I sensed him moving in the house next door. And thought he moved closer to me. In the early morning, I swayed to his tread on the stairs.

And thus a month passed. In the reality of working hours and weeks I moved seemingly unchanged through thirty days of time. And no one seemed to notice the filigree of colour, shape and features that traced themselves over my face and body.

They saw and heard only Bethesda Barnet. And believed her to be the Bethesda Barnet they had always known.

FIFTEEN

"I long for you, Bethesda."

"I am here, Samuel."

We walked towards the gates of Grantleigh Manor; this was our walk. As though we possessed the landscape. Samuel Keans, a farmer broad and hirsute, brown-eyed with skin painted by sun and wind, an ochre-coloured man, knew that the land could reward or punish him. Therefore he walked more lightly than his weight would imply, as though wary.

In his voice that day I detected an undernote of fear.

"I long to marry you, Bethesda. I long to walk this walk and know we will return to our own home where we will be constantly together. I long . . ."

". . . Such longing, Samuel. You have not been so outspoken before."

"But you always knew my intentions, Bethesda."

"A woman can often be sadly wrong in assuming she

understands what is unspoken. Particularly when it is the man who does not speak.''

"I'm speaking now, Bethesda. Will you honour me. . . ?''

"Ah, Samuel, it is you who honour me. An honour long hoped-for by my mother and perhaps long feared by your father.''

"My father admires you greatly, Bethesda. Why, only yesterday he informed me that Lord Grantleigh had expressed much admiration for your painting.''

"Such an accolade from Lord Grantleigh must have done little to dissipate your father's fears. I know nothing of farming; I teach and I paint. Hardly what he can have hoped for in a daughter-in-law.''

"Don't mock, Bethesda. He fears for you as much as for me.''

"And what has alleviated all that fear, Samuel? Lord Grantleigh's praise?''

"Today I have asked you to marry me, Bethesda. This conversation is not what I expected.''

"In what way?''

"It is puzzling . . . and in some way, sad.''

Samuel could sometimes surprise me. He spoke as though another man lay beneath the mass of him, a man I did not know. But then he knew nothing of his hoped-for wife, who had once so hoped for him. From foreground he had been moved to another position on the canvas, important structurally to the overall effect but no longer the very purpose of the work.

I could play with words now, with Samuel. I had the power that comes with secret knowledge and the delights of deception made me lighter in my dealings with him. His slightly puzzled look elicited no sweet kindness from me, as I carefully noted each stage of his confusion. I did not, however, allow myself to so abuse my power that I would risk losing a key figure in the edifice which was my surface life.

"Is it that you fear the loss of your teaching post?"

Upon marriage female teachers were obliged to vacate their post. Though, in my case, I thought it would be possible for me to give certain periods of extra tuition during the school year. Lord Grantleigh's passion for art was well known by the school and I was aware that Mr Slope would acquiesce to the slightest request from his patron.

No, Samuel, you have misinterpreted. It gave me satisfaction to think but not speak this line.

"Lord Grantleigh could perhaps . . ."

"No, Samuel, that is not my fear."

"Is it fear for your mother? I've always told you,

Bethesda, of my admiration of your kindness to your mother. A room is available in our home for her. She would be welcomed, I assure you.''

"No, Samuel, *that* is not my fear. You have always been generous in this respect."

"Then what is your answer, Bethesda? Will you marry me?"

"I know my answer, Samuel. But I need some time to adjust to the fact that you have asked the question."

"At last, Bethesda?"

"Ah, Samuel, now you mock me. But yes, at last."

It was a strange answer to a proposal but correct. Samuel and I had, just for a moment, found our common language. A mutual closing of doors against intimacy but done gently and with some wit.

Later, as expected, my mother's voice . . .

SIXTEEN

"Bethesda?"

"Yes, Mother?"

"Samuel has spoken?"

"Yes, Mother."

"Ah, at last."

"Yes, at last, Mother."

She did not smile.

"It is what you have long wanted."

"Well, long waited for, Mother."

Then suddenly, "Will you be happy with Samuel, Bethesda?"

A question which perhaps should have been posed years ago.

"Were you happy in marriage, Mother?"

"Happier than I would have been outside it."

"How can you know?"

"I know. And I would not have had you."

"Am I the only joy you found in it?"

"Oh no, Bethesda. I liked the look of my husband."

It seemed a time for frankness. Though I noticed she did not say "your father".

"Marriage. Marriage, at last. Your father would have been pleased. He knew Samuel as a young man . . ."

"He is still a young man, Mother."

"He is your age, Bethesda. He is thirty, is he not?"

"Yes, Mother."

"A long courtship is hard on a man."

With the announcement of Samuel's proposal, it was clear that I had entered a new state in life. One in which my mother could now speak to me with an openness bordering on indelicacy – a note which she had never struck before.

"The timing was of his choosing, Mother."

"Maybe."

"You know his father's worries. Their responsibilities to the farm. My inexperience."

"And the hope, Bethesda, that Samuel might marry into land."

An old fear arose in me. And an old anger. My mother was referring to Alice Thomas, whose father's farm lay close to Samuel's. Through the death of her brother, Alice had become its heir. I had wept for

Daniel Thomas when he died and shamefully a little for myself. He was eighteen and had been crushed beneath the wheels of his carriage. He had melded into the earth he had so carefully tended. It was a boy's death, a sudden commingling of machinery, earth and boyhood.

Death, on the occasions I had observed it before, simply rearranged peacefully the contours of the face. With gentle brush strokes it painted a final still-life, erasing at the corners of the mouth and eyes the disfiguring and futile contortions of the last moments. But, though I had not witnessed it, I knew Daniel Thomas' death was different. Violent. Bloody. Warlike. But then few women witnessed death on the battlefield. And men, perhaps ashamed, rarely wrote of how death in battle mauls, maims and unmakes them, obscenely. We are separate, men and women, in this long history of how we die.

After Daniel Thomas' death, an unmarried daughter with land lived adjacent to the Keans' family farm. And knowing Samuel better than he knew himself, I also knew that he was not so foolish as to be unaware of the change fate had wrought on the landscape of his county, and potentially of his life. His neighbours' tragedy presented to him a significant opportunity, through marriage, to increase for generations his family's patrimony. And farming families are ever seduced by the promise of land.

Samuel's father having only one son must have wished to persuade this son to look eastwards to Alice Thomas rather than south to the village and to me. There was a time, a little while ago, when, perhaps incorrectly, I thought Samuel called on me less often . . .

"Well, Mother, it would seem that Samuel's love of land has not overwhelmed him."

"Alice will be sad . . ."

"He never called on Alice Thomas."

"He did not need to. Alice is his neighbour. To be seen daily."

"Yes. Of course, you're right, Mother. But I think you understand me. Samuel has long been walking out with me."

"Very long. And I'm glad it's at an end."

"You haven't asked me for my reply, Mother."

"Bethesda, don't mock me."

"Ah, Mother, I would not mock my future. I will go to my room to think."

"Bethesda!"

"I will be down in an hour, Mother, to prepare supper."

"Bethesda. I did not mean . . ."

I sat before the image of Mathew Pearson's face which mirrored mine and we spoke a little. Like lovers. Those who do not have imaginary conversations do not love. The unspoken words that fall and flow are simply a world made word. Other conversations which we consider real are pale echoes of our secret speech. They are only games of hide and seek within a maze of sound.

"Your face, Mathew Pearson, is the face that I will think of when I die."

I smiled at him as I spoke.

"Your rain-drenched face, white and silver, is what will draw me on and on to whatever else is to be seen when I leave this world, Mathew. Draw me to you, Mathew. Draw me, Mathew, as I have drawn you. I feel as if your face must absorb me and devour me. When the time comes."

I walked a little with the image of him in my hand. Round and round in my dark room.

"Where can I keep you, Mathew, when I marry Samuel? You're married, Mathew. It's a life with a structure. A finished thing. Framed, Mathew. Marriage is a life defined and framed. And I think I need to be framed.

"Before I saw your face, Mathew, Samuel's pleased

me well enough. It still pleases. It is not that I see yours when I look at Samuel. It is that it has become just Samuel's face, with no other meaning. A man's face of pleasing proportions but one which has no other force beyond what I see. Samuel's face is information to me, only information."

There are those who pray to images. Who find a light in the Virgin's eyes which soothes them in their misery. And those who wish to kiss the feet of Christ on The Cross when grief overwhelms them. And His polished and painted cold feet with their tiny, jewel-red wounds cool their anger. I did no differently here. Idolatry? A sin to worship anyone other than God? What arrogance. And, besides, to those who are believers, who made Mathew Pearson's face?

To Mathew Pearson I whispered, spoke and sang a secret language every moment of the day and night. I had joined a long line, a many-coloured weaving pattern, of those called to worship. I was blessed. I was chosen. I was blessed that I was chosen.

SEVENTEEN

A child was dead. A day by the river had turned into tragedy. The schoolchildren were in a state of wonder. He who was, was no longer.

"Where is he, Miss Barnet?"

"Heaven. He is in Heaven, children."

They believed. The mother, whose name they knew but could only then think of as "his mother", this creature was causing terror in the village. Her rage was extreme.

The children looked at her in awe. Madness excited them. Their fear was delicious to them and she was not their mother. She was a mother and was now a mother without a child. They could not comprehend this. Nor could she.

The night of the drowning, I dreamed I saw her floating beneath me as I swam, not in a dark, muddy river but in a clean, warm sea. She smiled at me and pointed to some rocks. I swam towards them and there lay Robert, sleeping. His body seemed to float on a silver sheath of tiny fishes which almost breathed for him. They fluttered round the sleeping sweetness of his boy's body, shivers of busy nurses glimmering with watery life. I did not paint this dream. And have often wondered why.

The next day the headmaster, Mr Slope, addressed us.

"Robert has left us. God has called him. Robert heard God and responded. We who have not yet been called weep for Robert to come back to us. But we call him back from God. Children, this is not our right. We must desist from this. We must let Robert go to God. We must let Robert be with God. And we must ourselves patiently wait for God to call us. Robert is now in Heaven. We, alas, are still here on earth. But we must go on following the path laid out before us, mindful of our duty before a just and loving God. Robert's favourite subject was English and, as you know, he had a particular love of poetry. Mr Pearson our new English master will now speak to you."

Mathew Pearson spoke kindly. I found his speech did not influence my vision of him. Perhaps my vision of him was so profound that it drowned the sense of hearing. As one sense often drowns the other. As vision often dulls our hearing, and surrender to music can blind us to our surroundings.

"Today, children, I think of a boyhood friend of mine who died many years ago, when he was the same age as Robert. His name was Sean. He was Irish and only eight when he died of influenza. At that time I lived in the city, and could only rarely visit his grave, which was some way from my school and house. However, live in a village and, as the school and churchyard are close together, each day you will pass the graveyard where Robert lies. Each year on the anniversary of Robert's death we shall pray at his grave. So the geography of Robert's life and death is as known to you as all his history. And in that precious knowledge he will be long remembered. I have some lines of poetry, children, which we shall learn by heart later. They are sad lines. Today it is right and proper to be sad.

> *My tale was heard, and yet it was not told;*
> *My fruit is fall'n, and yet my leaves are green;*
> *My youth is spent, and yet I am not old;*
> *I saw the world, and yet I was not seen:*
> *My thread is cut, and yet it is not spun;*
> *And now I live, and now my life is done.*

THE STILLEST DAY

I sat to the left of Mathew Pearson as he addressed the school. A limited vision. As my eyes filled with tears, I cast them down to hide my sudden confusion. A familiar, female occlusion. Almost against my will, I absorbed an image of his black shoes tight-laced, reflected in a sudden sunbeam on the dark wooden floor.

And I thought how in my own room I could study him with impunity. All the parts of him which now I possessed. From any angle that I wished. He was a series of *mises en trait*, a sudden-watered face, a hand and shoulder and a small protrusion of bone – enough for identification of a god.

That night I added to my collection. I painted an image of the unknown skin and bones of his feet. Then on the naked skin I painted laced-tight coils of shiny black. And meticulously I executed intricate loops of blue-black to represent the knots which fell in gentle declaration to light, silk-tipped points.

Man's naked feet were nailed when I first saw them as a child. It is the same for many children. The thin bones of His feet pierced by metal and the eternally-dropping blood, more directly in our sight-line than the rest of His body. To kiss that image was usual, though sickening to me. I did not kiss the image of Mathew Pearson's feet but I did lay my face on the laces.

"Shall I tell stories to the image of your feet, Mathew?" I whispered.

"My name is Bethesda Barnet. I am twenty-nine years old. Soon to be thirty. What does age mean to you, Mathew? A woman's age? I see my face laced into your feet. Laced foot traced along my cheek bone, drawn on the surface of my white skin. This pallor is not becoming to me and would be better suited to one with dark hair. My hair is the fiercest thing about me – don't you think, Mathew? Look. Look, as I incline my head a little so that your feet are almost dancing on my hair. Samuel says my hair is a bursting bundle of waves and curls. For Samuel, that's a romantic description. I pin it tight in the day to calm its disorder. Some call me fair. But I think my hair has more the look of unpolished silver. There is something flat in it which, with my pallor, is unattractive.

"It is a fraught relationship, Mathew. The one which exists between me and my hair. There's great ferocity on both sides. It is not that I would wish for darker hair nor indeed for Mary's golden curls. Do you love her golden hair, Mathew?

"Does she, your Mary, lay her face upon your feet?

The Stillest Day

They say that Magdalen dried The Lord's feet with her hair. I would do that for you, Mathew. I have long hair, Mathew. Let me lay my hair upon the image of your feet. Dare I let you see it loose? Now, like this? Take care, Mathew. We both know that hair flowing loose before a stranger's eyes is a symbol of surrender. But yours are not stranger's eyes. Their outline on this other mirror is familiar to me now. And I am most familiar to myself when I am reflected through your eyes. Since that first day.

"I want to see myself as you see me. Is that what the mirror does? Arouse our own desire for ourselves in order to comprehend the desire of the other? *Desire?* Where do these words come from?"

Echoes of Lord Grantleigh floated into my mind describing a painting which had just arrived from his mother's house in France.

"See, Miss Barnet, how the artist implies that in ecstasy man's fury is tamed and put to use. For woman's pleasure. I myself have found that women do not understand this aspect of the male."

Lord Grantleigh's words faded away. He was a man who perhaps taught me certain things it was better not to know.

"Do you ever speak as Lord Grantleigh does,

Mathew? I think not, Mathew. How do you speak to Mary? Who taught you?

"Shall I tell you something, Mathew? I do not believe you speak much to Mary. She laughs and twinkles so, how could one interrupt or lessen such a flow and glow of happiness. No. No, best to smile and listen and remain quite silent."

As I swayed in my darkening room every fading point of light was to me a particle of Mathew Pearson. As though he had been shattered into fragments of stars which fell upon my mirror where they floated as silver leaves on the water. And the points of light wove themselves together and I spoke to a shimmering image. In whispers, as one should.

"It was your mother, Mathew, who encouraged you to marry. Did she frighten you into marriage? Oh, Mathew, you were trapped, were you not, by a mother? As we all are. She lost a daughter and wanted another. Predatory. They're all predatory.

"She wanted Mary who so resembled her dead daughter to be beside her for life. And in order to achieve that, with careful, maternal cunning she placed her beside you, Mathew. For it was her desire that was achieved when you married Mary. It was not your desire at all, was it, Mathew? It was your mother's. Mothers are the same with sons as with daughters. Forever plotting. It is a state of being. They are afraid that we may learn to move away from them finally. So they guide us towards their chosen exit which is never truly the way out. It is just another door they open for us into a room they have designed.

"If I had just one part of you I would spend a lifetime in its worship. To have all of you might cause such terror in me. Where, where to begin? Your feet I have imagined so am more at ease with them. And could lace myself up tight with black and silver cord for you to open with your thumb bent slightly back, as it always is.

"Then your thumb could press out my eyes. Press out here and now and press me deep into other realms, where darkness is followed by the sudden explosion of diminishing rings of light. So, I press like this with my own thumb and still I can see you. You are painted on the mirrored image of the world which we carry with us when we sleep.

"You're safe within me, Mathew. I will carry you wherever I go. To Samuel's house. For that is surely waiting for me. And then you and I will look south to my old home, as I once looked north and waited for

Samuel. Waited to have my life shaped to the constraints of others.''

As I look upon these carved and vaulted walls which enclose me now, as they have for many years, I know that I had always feared the unfettered self. And had therefore restrained it within a disciplined rigidity. Perhaps I had hoped that as the blue-flowered agapanthus flourishes best when compressed in tightly-potted soil, so I too would blossom in constraint.

EIGHTEEN

Lord Grantleigh fulfilled his duties to the village in his own eccentric manner. Sensitive to much in art, he was capable of brutality in life. As Robert died in the river which ran through Lord Grantleigh's estate, I had been requested to decorate a small iron seat which would stand in Grantleigh Park in Robert's memory. It would mark the spot at which he had slipped and succumbed to the river's cold embrace. Too easily, I thought. Surely he could have fought harder and clutched at the river's bank. But then a child's mind floats with death more often than we like to think.

"I do not know myself to be capable of the task, Lord Grantleigh."

"Now, Miss Barnet, I feel certain you will not disappoint me in this."

In the conservatory his tall, etiolated body paced in some agitation to and fro from a veritable forest of miniature ferns across the stone floor to a high, thin eucalyptus which seemed to mirror his shape.

". . . You are capable of any task. Particularly one set by me."

"As ever, Lord Grantleigh."

"As ever, Miss Barnet."

"Why do you want to do this?"

"My river needs absolution."

"Are you suggesting it has sinned, Lord Grantleigh?"

"My dear Miss Barnet, absolution is a daily requirement for most of us, heathen or priest."

"You have a fine conscience, Lord Grantleigh."

"Just perfect vision, Miss Barnet."

"Perfect vision?"

"Of my soul. Anyone who requires less than daily absolution is simply suffering from moral cataracts."

"I must aim for clearer vision . . ."

"The artist, Miss Barnet, rarely has a clear vision of himself."

"Or herself."

"Great art is beyond gender. Now to the subject of poor Robert's bench. Shall we celebrate what he enjoyed of life or mourn what he has lost?"

"As you are the patron, you must decide."

THE STILLEST DAY

"A celebration, Miss Barnet. A glorious celebration. Do you agree?"

The decision, his decision, had been taken. Relieved, he sat down. And his body, fern-framed in pinnate fronds, rested on a vivid, red-lacquered bamboo chair. The spoils of yet another trip. And had I painted the scene, I would have emphasised the startling, almost bizarre contrast between the subdued colouring of his English gentleman's dress and the exotically-hued oriental chair.

"I am a little shocked."

"Don't be, Miss Barnet. Any life for any time. One just wants the experience. Whatever it means. Would you be shocked if I suggested yellow?"

"Yellow?"

"Yes. Yellow. But fierce."

"A yellow bench will be fierce indeed on the green path, Lord Grantleigh."

"Yes, but everyone will know that Robert was here. That's all we need. Someone to notice we were here. We're decided then, Miss Barnet. Yellow."

"Yellow then, Lord Grantleigh. Have you spoken to his mother?"

"Yes. She's pleased, I think, about the seat. But I never truly know what people feel about . . ."

"Beneficence?"

"The giver can compel acceptance. Particularly in my case. And in these sad circumstances compulsion is inappropriate. Will you speak to her on the subject of colour?"

"It is so hard to speak of colour to her now. One cannot comprehend the colour of her despair."

"Could you paint despair, Miss Barnet?"

"Perhaps."

"But the eye of the about-to-be satisfied lover might gaze upon it and see hope. Interpretation lies in the eye of the beholder, Miss Barnet, as it looks out from the landscape of individual experience and expectation."

"Or of dreams, Lord Grantleigh. Art is understood best in that landscape. And Robert's mother will often see him in dreams. Though not, I think, dressed in yellow."

"Miss Barnet, even a conversation such as this has an enchantment. Do you speak to Mr Samuel Keans like this? I doubt it. The Bishop informs me that we may expect an announcement soon."

"I had little idea the Bishop had any interest in my affairs. Other than spiritual, of course."

"Ah well, an interest in the spiritual affairs of one's congregation . . ."

"Flock. He refers to them as his flock."

"It is remarks like that, Miss Barnet, which make me so enjoy our Thursday meetings. But you've not answered my question concerning your conversations with Mr Keans. . . ?"

"We have lately developed a quite adequate language. No . . . more than adequate."

"For a lifetime's conversation, Miss Barnet?"

"Perhaps, perhaps."

"Ah, so you will soon surrender then?"

I remained silent.

"I forbid you to change your life so drastically that our Thursdays are no more."

This, with his most deceptive smile.

Again I remained silent.

There was a slight awkwardness. Then, with a sigh:

"Miss Barnet, if you would care to follow me to my study . . . Some journals have arrived from Paris. Since my last visit I have given long consideration to certain new artists whose work has been brought to my attention by my mother. She has an intrepid soul and so lights upon the extreme, undaunted. These journals contain reproductions and articles which I should like to discuss with you."

The note in his voice was not unduly imperative.

However, like everyone in the village, I felt it best to follow where Lord Grantleigh led. As I walked the length of the conservatory behind him, I traced through the low-pitched slightly opaque roof the durable lace shadows of its cast-iron decoration. Wordlessly, we continued through the connecting passage with its curvilinear trellis to his study.

It was a tactful room to which no eastern ferocity of colour provided an unsettling counterpoint. It contained echoes of the conservatory in its dry-grass green needlework settee and in the hangings of trailing foliage which fell ceiling to floor on either side of the carved wood mantelpiece.

On the old English oak desk an urn-shaped clock ticked discreetly. Beside the clock, in two meticulously neat stacks, lay journals entitled *L'Ymagier* and *Le Symboliste.* And a book, *Certains* by J.K. Huysmans.

"Do sit down, Miss Barnet."

Lord Grantleigh drew up a chair beside his own.

"I would like your comments, Miss Barnet."

He opened the journal and I believed I saw a leopard with a female face caress the naked body of a young man, their heads a wash of Venetian gold.

Silence.

He turned the pages. A single, human eye rose on a

bloom of white cloud towards the sky as though it travelled towards infinity. Trembling, I stood up.

"I find these paintings impossible, Lord Grantleigh."

"Impossible?"

"Yes. Just that. Impossible."

And though I knew my arbitrary tone strained the fine line that separated us, I was helpless. It was as though my mind was assaulted by an irresistible effusion of images. Abnormal images clouding and crowding, effecting a transmutation of all that I had ever seen before.

"There is another reality, Miss Barnet. There *is* an elsewhere. The haunting and haunted landscape of the mind in dreams. A landscape in which all is possible. These new artists are its courageous cartographers. They are daring explorers. We owe them a debt of gratitude."

"Forgive me, Lord Grantleigh, may I have a glass of water?"

"My dear Miss Barnet. Of course. It is I who should apologise to you. Perhaps I was unwise . . ."

He poured into a clear glass clear water. Nothingness of colour, contained.

"No. No, Lord Grantleigh. Perhaps it is simply that I'm too distressed by Robert's death to be fully receptive to what it is that you have shown me."

"We're both distressed by Robert's death, Miss Barnet. This was not the most opportune time . . . I had forgotten how disturbing these paintings are when one first sees them."

As though to rescue me, we returned to an old conversation concerning The Rules of Taste; within which more safety lay. As he had often explained, their application was a mirror to the spirit of the age.

"My great-grandfather followed them when he built Grantleigh Manor in 1740. Have you noticed, Miss Barnet, there is no tension in this house between interior and exterior? There are of course those who devote themselves to one or t'other – a dangerous choice. For whether it is interior or exterior which dominates, the price is eternal conflict and contention."

"Did your grandfather live his life according to The Rules of Taste?"

"I'm no longer certain, Miss Barnet, that such a thing is possible. Or perhaps my own vision has been altered. My mother is a dangerous influence. No wonder she returned to Paris on my father's death . . ."

He continued quickly, agitatedly, as though anxious to communicate the incommunicable.

"Now she tells me that I too may begin to 'love what never has been'. And she has given me a book in which the hero maintains that he is only interested in works of art which are 'inflamed, or fevered, or already wasting away' . . . Do you feel better now, Miss Barnet?''

"Thank you, Lord Grantleigh, yes."

"Again, forgive me if I have distressed you in any way. Perhaps we can discuss these works at a later date.

" 'Inflamed and fevered art', Lord Grantleigh, is that from *Certains*?''

"No, Miss Barnet, though it is by the same author."

He picked up the book, flicked through and quoted:

" '. . . a body of solemn grace inhabited by a soul worn out with solitary ideas and secret thoughts.' ''

He looked at me.

"When I read that line I thought of you, Miss Barnet. Though the full quotation is not at all suitable."

"Since I don't read French, Lord Grantleigh, I doubt that I will ever know the full quotation."

"Life will teach you that all we know is never all there is. A point often made to me by my mother."

"She seems to have had great influence on you, Lord Grantleigh. As mothers always have."

"I could have done nothing with my life other than take care of my estates and hunt, had not my mother's ferocious dedication to art shaped me from childhood.

Let us change the subject. Do you intend to keep Mr Keans waiting?''

"I am a little confused at the moment, Lord Grantleigh.''

"May I advise you, my dear? And in order to do so I must speak frankly. And in speaking frankly, I take a great risk. But if I am wrong in my assessment of your character, Miss Barnet, I am wrong in everything.''

I said nothing.

"Marriage, Miss Barnet, is often simply a long recrimination for the errors of courtship. I made such errors, and paid for them long ago. And pay still. For the narrow pass of marriage allows but one person to squeeze through. To be burdened with guilt makes for a most uncomfortable journey. And I had misread my companion. My wife is Irish, Miss Barnet. I met her at a hunt. She terrified and fascinated me. That wild, black hair, common enough in her own country but still extraordinary to me. The constant threat of violence from her tiny frame. A small body and a small intellect, and certainly not one that leans towards art. Of course, in fairness, it is impossible to lean towards art. One is either consumed or not.''

I did not make the error here of questioning him. I would follow his every word but allow myself no expression of interest, for fear of deflecting him from a subject which had long fascinated me, the mysterious marriage of Lord and Lady Grantleigh.

"Oh, my errors were the normal errors a man might make, believing the matter settled with his bride. Believing that he could with impunity pursue his pleasures to the last moment. And sometimes beyond. I am a man, and had wished to keep certain aspects of myself from my wife-to-be."

I was not certain whether to be angry or grateful for this excessive candour. I remained silent.

"But she discovered me. And she had her revenge. The Irish cannot breathe without revenge. There is no mercy in them. She hunted to the first child's destruction. The second pregnancy she brought to term. My daughter Arabella. And then she gave me George.

" 'You're now endowed with daughter and son, sir,' she said to me. 'And I have finished with this marriage business and will hunt my time away. You were a fool, Grantleigh, to imagine my forgiveness possible. Enjoy yourself where you may.'

"Would any man not adore such a fiend, Miss Barnet? She broke my will. Magnificently. While at the same time binding me to her forever. With children, Miss

Barnet. Women! The playwright was correct. 'Women Beware Women.' ''

"Mothers . . . Lord Grantleigh. Beware mothers.''

"Perhaps with Mr Keans you wish to balance your life. All that is interior and hidden and which I cannot fathom you may now wish to house differently. According to which rules, Miss Barnet?''

"Perhaps the rules of necessity, Lord Grantleigh. I imagine you are less familiar with them than I.''

I knew that I had gone too far.

"Miss Barnet, we must finish. Perhaps we have gone too far today. For which of course you are naturally entirely to blame.'' He smiled at me.

"My final words of advice on the subject of Mr Keans. Do not go to him. Wait. But when he comes, pounce, Miss Barnet. Settle this matter with speed. So that then we can put it away forever. Mr Keans, and your relationship with him, must not in future be allowed to intrude on our magnificent Thursdays. It will be some time before I forgive you.''

I allowed this lie. "Some day I hope you will, Lord Grantleigh.''

Everything had changed between Lord Grantleigh and me. And we both now were anxious to lighten the conversation in a vain pretence that this was not so. I left him quietly with practised deference.

As I made my way home, into the landscape of my mind floated a single, stripped eye. Which gazed down as though mesmerised on the enigmatic human face of an amorous leopard. And, onto the topography with which I was so familiar, this strange vision painted itself and seemed to me more real than the woods and fields through which I'd walked since I was a child.

As I recall them now in my years of grave seclusion, my Thursdays with Lord Grantleigh were suffused with an air of gaiety. Life's players add more to our experience than we ever know. They weave a giddy wonder and the air is light around them. And brighter, lighter still to those who look at them from the dark.

NINETEEN

"Bethesda! Bethesda!"

My mother. The note was high. I was in my room. I was with Mathew Pearson. We were dancing. The image of his face blending into my own.

"Bethesda! Mary is here."

The mind music stopped.

"Your wife is here, Mathew. I must leave you. I will wrap you carefully in my silver shawl and place you . . ."

"Bethesda!"

"Coming, Mother. Coming."

Mary Pearson stood awkwardly large in our small sitting room. A disproportionate figure. I wondered that she did not tear, her skin being pulled so tight. She moved forward in a swinging motion. Her legs pushed farther apart than modesty would permit to the unmarried woman.

THE STILLEST DAY

Mary Pearson's sanctioned pregnancy forced her into the manoeuvres of the old and obese whose stomachs dictate the angle of approach. An approach which is then culminated by an indecorous collapse into a chair.

Her breathing was shallow.

"May I," she gasped, "speak frankly? I am now so large at eight months I scarcely know that I can survive till nine months have passed. Oh, dear me. I did not suppose it could be like this, so heavy. So heavy."

"But we never carry a more worthwhile burden, Mary dear."

Mary Pearson smiled assent. And they were silent, the mothers, and content.

I was revolted. I had once been contained within my mother. This old woman. So thin now that one could believe a heavy meal would place too great a burden on her stomach. For months I had been trapped, unable to get out. What was trapped within Mary Pearson? Mathew Pearson's child. I had no wish for such a gift. What is it that I wished for? An endless, silent idolatry. The image of my Lord will fill my room and life and I will spend my time there in adoration.

"Bethesda, there is a little story carried by a singing bird from Farmer Keans . . ."

My mother smiled and tapped one hand upon the other in arthritic applause.

Such a sweet and dainty face your wife has, Mathew. And such sweet and dainty words. I did not speak my thoughts.

"Bethesda must answer you, Mary. My lips are sealed."

They laughed. It was a kind of female laughter which I detested. Lord Grantleigh and I had sometimes noted the veritable witch-like quality of the consensual laughter of women.

"Is it to be, Bethesda?"

I remained silent.

"Just think, Mrs Barnet, in a few years' time my child and Bethesda's may play together."

It was true. It was the nature of it all. "Yes," to Samuel. That one word would bring all in its wake. And, "No." What was there for me, then, should I say no?

"Come now, Bethesda. Mary is our friend and discreet."

"I think it unwise, Mother, to speak of this before I speak to Samuel."

It was an unflattering reality that Mary Pearson looked shocked that I should hesitate to accept Samuel's proposal. Clearly I was perceived differently from how I perceived myself. "It was ever thus," Lord Grantleigh would remark. I liked the phrase. It tolled. And went on tolling. As certain as the school bells which structured my time, and as invariable.

"Forgive me, Bethesda. Everyone longs to hear of a marriage. It can be hard on the couple. I remember when Mathew and I . . ."

And was no doubt very hard on you, madam. My secret thoughts were becoming more brutal.

"Were your parents very anxious that you should wed?"

The words were out in little vicious notes, they posed a question that seemed to . . .

"My parents died when I was young . . ."

Defeated. A little sting of grief, Lord Grantleigh says, is homeopathy for the soul. "We need it, Miss Barnet. Reminds us we are human and therefore mortal."

". . . My brother and I were but ten and twelve. He went to stay with my uncle for a time and I was blessed that Mathew's mother took me to live with them."

My mother looked at me as though she was ashamed of me. My mother to whom gossip was mother's milk. The injustice and disloyalty of her reaction made me rage against her. It was a hidden rage.

"Mathew's home was like my own after that."

"A long friendship." My mother spoke kindly. Her head moved stiffly up and down nodding her approval of how that young friendship had led to a new life. Just life. Unspecific. Amorphous. New, like spring. A renewal of what we had thought dead in winter.

I moved slightly away from these women who knew so much more than me, much of which I did not wish to know.

A portrait of Mary Pearson would now have been almost impossible to execute. She moved constantly in a frantic search for ease. And each manoeuvre was accompanied by a fleeting change of expression as hope of comfort turned to disappointment and then to serene resignation. To catch Mary Pearson's exact likeness now so that one could say, "Ah, that is how she is. Or how she was," it would be necessary to paint imperturbable stillness beneath an agitation of activity.

"Some tea, Mary?"

"You're very kind, Mrs Barnet. However, I would prefer water."

"You are ill, my dear?"

Are we all dying of thirst, Mother, that water instantly soothes us?

"I must not be ill."

THE STILLEST DAY

"What do you mean, Mary. . . ?" My mother's voice, drenched in solicitude.

"Mothers must not become ill. It is dangerous. It is dangerous for the baby. And later for the child. It is terrible to be left motherless."

And I thought, "Don't sting me with your grief, madam. I am immune."

"Will you forgive me, Mary. I must return to my room, Mother. I have some work to prepare for tomorrow."

My mother voiced no dismay that I should leave them. Indeed it seemed to me that she and Mary moved closer to each other with an eager tenderness from which I felt excluded. And as I mounted the stairs I thought, "I am hot, I am very hot." Almost desperate with longing I closed the door. I cradled the mirror with his face upon it and moved to and fro as though we danced.

"I need to be scattered all over your face, Mathew. And you over mine. I want to be refracted, reflected. And then cooled by the first vision of you." I did not whisper but simply breathed the words.

Echoes of Lord Grantleigh . . .

"Copulation, Miss Barnet, is for animals. It is the base line of sexuality. Speedy. Often satisfying. Then over.

There are, however, those gifted in what is in fact an art form. They know the endless pleasure, indeed the endless pressure of choice. The rest is just imperative.''

His voice faded. I took my face away. Copulation complete. He was right. It was contemptible.

''I will from now on not touch you, Mathew. I will only gaze.'' I promised. And if there was sound it was but a rustle or a sigh . . .

''Bethesda! Bethesda! Mary is leaving.''

''Coming, Mother. Coming.''

The blonde pygmy and her giant stomach were leaving. Perhaps my mother soothed her for she fluttered less, physically and verbally. She was more calm. Becalmed. Not a dead calm. She was becalmed by life.

I took her elbow, angled sharp in all this roundness. And I found she rested upon my arm as though she trusted it.

''Forgive my prying, Bethesda, I really was indiscreet. Forgive me, please. We married ones want everyone to join our state.''

''Is it so wonderful then?''

''It is so wonderful. Aah . . .''

She tripped a little on the step up to the front door. Did I misguide her? I thought not. The door opened.

''Mathew!'' She almost cried his name.

THE STILLEST DAY

His arms reached towards her.

"Mary, you look so pale. Are you. . . ?"

"It is nothing, Mathew. Bethesda has been so kind and helped me to the door."

"And in a moment you'll be home. Such a short journey. We are so lucky that you and your mother live beside us, Miss Barnet. Particularly now."

"Though Bethesda may be about to . . ."

She stopped. He smiled at me. Full face. But then I could make his face fill any space. The sky was darkening. If he would but wait, rain would splash on his face. As it did when I first saw him.

"Miss Barnet will most surely be here in a month's time when the baby is born. Will you not, Miss Barnet?"

"I feel certain I will."

"You do not know how much that pleases me. Ah . . . the rain. Let's get you inside, Mary. You must not get wet now . . ."

The rain splashed down on my own face as I turned to my door, alone. And my own rain-sodden face was not the vision I had wanted. Nor did I see it as I walked down my mirrorless hall towards my mother.

"She will find it hard, that baby."

"From what you've told me it is always hard, Mother."

"Bethesda, I did not fill you with old wives' tales."

"No. Only old mothers' tales, Mother. But few, I grant you."

She gazed at me. Perhaps she tried to see the womb behind my covered stomach. And my stomach felt tight and hot. And I would not soothe it. I decided that that night I would be mirrorless.

TWENTY

Samuel's hand was on my face. Skin to skin. I felt the slight pressure and the uneven dryness of his fingertips. What is it to feel when only the body feels?

"Do you have an answer for me, Bethesda?"

One yes would lead to another and that yes would lead on to Mary Pearson's condition. Just yes . . .

"No, I do not yet have an answer."

"Why not?"

"I have much to think of, Samuel."

"As have I, Bethesda. When will you let me know? There's talk already in the village, Bethesda."

"Samuel, I too have long listened to talk as the years went by . . ."

"Is this my punishment, Bethesda?"

"Lord Grantleigh says we all have the desire to punish. We simply lack the power."

"Lord Grantleigh does not lack power. He was born with it."

"As were you. You were born to inherit your land as he was to inherit his. And I to inherit none."

"Our children would inherit."

"It's a long body, Samuel, stretching back over the land, one and one making one."

His hand moved from my covered breast. A permitted path. And now he tried for new ways and lanes to me.

This testing of boundaries was not a battle between us but an accepted ritual, almost a courtesy. These were old surrenders: that of clothed breast, and the incline I allowed. The slight arching and protruding that I undertook in order that he could rest himself against me. After which and trembling a little he would walk away from me to return minutes later and escort me home. Now our old familiar journey might be changed. A new destination which would alter everything. And I felt that everything was being pressed upon me, almost crushing me. As he had pressed upon me so desperately that evening. The intense physicality was obtrusive. I moved from our hidden position behind a tree on "our walk" which had afforded a longed-for privacy to village couples down the years. Purposefully, I turned towards home. Samuel was obliged to follow me.

"Why do you want to marry me?"

"Because I long for you more than for anyone."

"Have you longed for others, Samuel?"

"Sometimes."

"For. . . ?"

"Once, long ago, Bethesda."

"And why did you not proceed?"

"Because I saw you."

"But you have always seen me."

"That is all I can say, Bethesda. I saw you."

"Differently?"

"Differently."

"Is it possible, do you think, to see just once to know?"

"Anything is possible, Bethesda. We are near your house. Do not make me wait too long, I beg you. It hurts a man."

"It hurts a woman too."

"Tire of your punishment, Bethesda."

"Before you tire of me?"

"No. No, Bethesda."

Sunset. A sudden, lambent ray of winter sun and Mathew Pearson, bathed in light, seemed to step from it. To me he was a silver man and looked wrong painted by a wash of gold.

"Miss Barnet. Thank you for being so kind to Mary today . . . Good afternoon, Mr Keans."

"Mr Pearson."

As he bowed to Mathew Pearson, Samuel's moustache had never seemed to slash across his face so harshly, a cicatrice of hair. I supposed he must often swallow hair: a thought which had not occurred to me before.

Another echo of Lord Grantleigh . . .

"Did they eat her hair, Miss Barnet?" He had posed the question as we stood before a painting I disliked which hung in the hall of Grantleigh Manor. There was something cruel in the eyes of the young woman abstractedly brushing her golden river of hair. And a sadness in the eyes of the adoring swains as they gazed at her, mesmerised into almost sacrificial obeisance.

I had never eaten hair.

The two men remained silent, as though waiting for me to speak. The sun went in and Mathew Pearson's whiteness seemed suddenly to have the quality of clouds. Finally, he spoke.

"Have you had a nice walk, Miss Barnet? Mary finds it difficult now. We used to walk a lot."

Before marriage? As lovers walked? Fearful to stop and perhaps succumb. All that walking and waltzing before a lying down. I had waltzed with Mathew Pearson but had not walked with him. And would never lie beside him.

He inclined his head towards us as he left. And I knew that I would not pant to touch his hair were it the colour of gold. I must have a need for black which comes out of the long line of lovers who made me . . .

I wished for so little I told myself as Samuel and I walked towards my house. Simply the hair from his head. So little yet so impossible. Something of him that would be mine not to paint or gaze upon but to ingest. I knew that the compressive force of the stomach as it grinds was more powerful than many machines. A hair of his head. So little. A hair of his head to journey through me.

"He is a quiet one, that Mr Pearson."

"Yes."

"I like his wife, Mary. She smiles a lot. She has a sweet nature."

"I think so too."

"And soon to be a mother."

"There would seem little doubt of that, Samuel."

Life churned in Mary Pearson and all I longed for was one hair of Mathew Pearson's head.

Had Samuel said "let us marry", even a short time

ago, I would have believed I had all I wanted and would have been content.

"I often think of you as a mother, Bethesda."

"Do you, Samuel?"

"Yes, Bethesda."

And I thought suddenly of what was required for this to happen. And I knew how I would swell. How much more subtle would be just one hair from Mathew Pearson's head.

Do not groan, Samuel. I could hear such hunger underneath his voice. Was I there to sate it? Is that what I was? Water and food to Samuel? You could have been fed earlier had you been pressing in your suit.

"Bethesda, you must answer me soon. My father . . ."

"I am not to marry your father, Samuel."

"Bethesda, I acknowledge that I may have been tardy in my proposal but I am now weary of this. Yes or no? I have long longed for you. I have defied my father for you."

"As you should, Samuel. As you should."

"My God, I see something in you that I had not seen before."

"And what is that, Samuel?"

"Such anger, Bethesda."

THE STILLEST DAY

"And what causes such anger?"

"I must assume it's me, Bethesda."

"Perhaps."

"Then your feelings towards me are not as I believed them to be."

We were now outside my house. And as we stood for a moment not knowing whether to enter together and face my mother in a state of argument, Mary Pearson appeared, smiling and plump and drenched in motherhood, at her own door.

"Samuel! Bethesda! What a delight to see you both again."

She panted a little. Even short sentences seemed to strain her lungs. Which were no doubt forced high in her and slightly crushed by the baby. Foetus. The word had shocked me when I first heard it.

I tried to hide from Mary Pearson the sudden bitterness which had flared between Samuel and me. I was ashamed as unhappiness always shames us. Being unmarried, and therefore presumed needy, the failure to please would have been judged to be mine. I laid my hand upon Samuel's arm which tensed as he moved it slightly away. I felt this to be a betrayal. He would not dissemble in front of others. So I would always need to be careful and controlled with him.

And I felt like a thing at bay between them. The physical reality of Mary Pearson and Samuel intruded on my dream. And in order to protect my secret world certain obtrusive aspects of life might need to be sacrificed. And even then I knew this to be a dangerous choice.

"We have just met Mathew. Two Pearsons on one walk." I smiled.

"Soon to be three," said Samuel.

Is it necessary always to draw attention to the about-to-be-born? Do we think they, the foetus – oh, how that word disgusts me – will forget their invitation to arrive?

She looked at us. And sighed.

"It is a mysterious experience and will, I think, be mysterious to you, too, Bethesda, when the time comes."

Her remark was indiscreet. She knew this and blushed so that she became a pink orb. Everything about her seemed beneficent and full of light and life.

"Mathew had an appointment with Mr Slope. I was to come a little later as Mrs Slope has invited us both to supper."

"May I accompany you, Mary? Bethesda must now attend to her mother."

I was dismissed, punished. Samuel would walk beside

this circular creature. Perhaps she would simply roll forward and he would need to restrain her?

"Of course, Samuel, you must accompany Mary."

I trod a fine line. I did not wish to simper, nor to be wholly unbending. My future lay before me, once much longed for, and even now much needed. I determined in that instant to say yes to Samuel. I could ride reality and dream side by side like two horses, tethered to the same carriage.

I did not turn to look at them as they walked away from me. I opened my door and waited to be called.

TWENTY-ONE

"Bethesda."

"Mother."

"Did you and Samuel have a nice walk?"

"Yes."

She was waiting for a decision. Everything she said to me now seemed to have within it a note of desperation. Hers must be deemed a shorter future than mine and she would like it settled.

"Did you speak at all of marriage?"

"Yes."

She sighed.

". . . Oh yes, of marriage and of children."

"And?"

"And I will speak to him finally tomorrow."

"Finally?"

"Yes, Mother."

"What does that mean, Bethesda?"

"I will say yes. Is that what you want to hear, Mother?"

"Thank God. Oh, thank God."

"God, Mother? Is He to be thanked that Samuel has spoken at last? If so, why did He delay so long in using His influence on Samuel?"

"Bethesda, may I speak to you more openly than I normally do?"

"I thought we were always truthful with each other."

"No, Bethesda, we are not."

"In what way are we untruthful?"

"Bethesda, you're nearly thirty years of age."

"And unmarried. I'm aware of that, Mother."

"Samuel delayed an inordinate time and that has harmed you."

"You have not been so vehement previously in your condemnation of him."

"I do not condemn him. He too has a future to consider. And he has a difficult and greedy father."

"I was not aware you knew Samuel's father so well."

"You are an artist, Bethesda. You're a dreamer and you believe you see more than others. But very often you do not. You are sometimes blind to what is very clear to others. But what you do see you see almost too deeply. As though in a dream. I am not a dreamer."

"And never have been, Mother."

"You know me less well than you imagine. But my past is not what I wish to discuss with you now. Let us concentrate on the dangers here to you, Bethesda."

"Dangers? What dangers? I will marry Samuel."

"Then tell him so speedily."

"He has not been asked to wait long, Mother."

"He believes it unnecessary that he should be asked to wait at all."

"And that makes me angry, Mother."

"At last you speak openly. Swallow your anger, Bethesda, in case you lose him."

"Lose him? Lose him?"

"Yes. Lose him."

"To whom?"

"To Alice Thomas."

I raged that she should so despise my powers with a man that she imagined he would leave me for Alice Thomas. And then I felt fear. Perhaps she was right. Perhaps I, who saw so much, whose eyes were seared by visions, saw nothing.

"Samuel will not marry Alice Thomas. He is betrothed to me."

"Not yet, Bethesda. You've not accepted him. He is still a free man."

THE STILLEST DAY

Barriers painstakingly erected over the years between my mother and myself were collapsing. Chaos, a demon sprite that I could almost see, was dancing around the house. Breaking things. Old taboos. Weakening the edifice that had let us live together for all this time. I wished to remove myself from this arena, from its fear and terror.

"I will not continue this conversation further, Mother."

"No doubt you will retire to your room and your painting, Bethesda."

"Do you envy me that, Mother?"

"Less than you might imagine, my dear."

I mounted the stairs and closed my door. And within seconds I had withdrawn into another reality. A blessed elsewhere. Where silently and secretly "I loved what never had been".

TWENTY-TWO

On the Wednesday before Ash Wednesday, I returned from school with a new vision of Mathew Pearson's mouth, curved in laughter, pocketed within my soul. My joy had an innocence. I felt as though I were a child hiding a precious pebble in her pocket. To touch and turn it round and round in the dark.

Lost in contemplation, I opened the door to my house and was assaulted by two voices which seemed to swoop and rise and fall about the house like trapped, hysterical birds. My mother's voice was a familiar intrusion in the hidden chambers of my mind. It was a voice against which over years I had still not built an adequate defence. The other voice was so light, I strained to catch the echo. Though I sensed a predatory note. I feared that Mary Pearson was breaking into my mind and stealing my thoughts: thoughts which I wished to savour in silence.

"Bethesda, will you help me? I dearly wish to show Mary the painting."

"The painting?"

"The painting which you gave your father when you left for . . ."

"But it's in your bedroom, Mother. And the stairs are so difficult for you and for Mary."

"Bethesda, I have decided that I have become too fearful. I don't walk enough. I'm too careful. And your mother is so proud of your painting. I would very much like to see it."

I turned to my mother, almost pleading with her.

"But you find the stairs so trying."

"Mary and I have just been discussing our frailties and are certain that we exaggerate them. Mothers sometimes do. Perhaps I've withdrawn too soon from certain aspects of life. Yes, I'm sure of it. Mary and I are going to be more daring. Come with me, Mary. Bethesda, your arm . . ."

Metamorphosis. Mary Pearson's obtrusive shape straining the boundaries of containment had a force which disturbed the agreed movements of the dance, the *pas de deux* my mother and I had practised so perfectly through the years. These women, these mothers, acted upon each other. There was an alchemy which subtly worked on them and which was beyond my control.

This cursed power to give life bred disgusting arrogance. They were forcing me to do their will. I was flooded with resignation to them. I felt I was suffocating. Surely this could not last long, this terrifying and enclosed time with them in which the energy that flowed between them effected some form of transmutation. Surely Mathew Pearson would soon arrive to remove this mountainous, rounded, pink and golden tumbling creature from my home. And the spell which seemed to work between them would be broken.

"Well, Mary, we are doing well. Half way up already. Thank you, Bethesda. How I have relied on your strength during all these years. Mary, if you have a daughter I pray she will be as good to you as my daughter has been to me. There! See, Bethesda! We're almost at the last stair. Victory, my dear Mary. I feel victorious."

"We've done very well, Mrs Barnet. But only because of Bethesda's help."

"There's Bethesda's room, Mary. Can we have a peep, my dear? Bethesda has an antique easel in her room given to her by Lord Grantleigh. It's Italian and rather valuable. He greatly appreciates Bethesda's work, my dear . . . Mary?"

"Forgive me, Mrs Barnet . . . May I rest for a moment? I have a slight ache in my left leg."

"Of course, my dear. You know, Mary, a mother's pride in her child's talent is perhaps a little vainglorious. Sometimes this pride can be almost sinful. Do you feel better now, Mary dear?"

"I think so, Mrs Barnet," she replied, breathing heavily.

We stopped again. A trinity of dark-skirted women, a triptych at the centre of which stood Mary Pearson. And at either side of this iconic creature, as though waiting to enfold her, were two tall, thin women. One slightly bowed by age.

And then we were gliding as though in a dream towards my room. My mother now with her hand on my arm and either exhausted or elated practising steps with which I felt suddenly unfamiliar. Behind us both, so close that the protrusion of her stomach almost touched the stuff of my dress, Mary Pearson followed.

My room was perfect in its pristine order. No aspect of Mathew Pearson gazed at his wife's reflection from displayed mirrors. Everything was hidden, shrouded in heavy drawers or curtained by skirts and dresses in my wardrobe.

"Why, Bethesda, how beautiful! How peaceful and calm your room is."

"Bethesda spends hours here alone painting, so . . . Mary? Mary?"

"I feel so strange. Something strange has occurred within me. Something has happened to me . . . in me . . . Oh dear! Oh Mathew! Mathew! Oh dear . . . I see. I can't see . . . What's there. . . ? What's there? Mathew . . . Oh, Mathew . . ."

Mary Pearson fell on the floor of my room. Suddenly. She did not even put her hand out to save herself. She made no movement with her arms even to save the child. Her huge body was felled. A strike by some unseen hand had simply cut her down.

"My God. Oh God, Bethesda! Oh what has happened to Mary . . . oh my God . . ."

And it is the stillest day. The Wednesday before Ash Wednesday. It is the stillest hour. I feel its stillness always, year after year, even now, years later. I will always feel its stillness. Each day before and every hour before and after has a rhythm, a confection of movement, a configuration of time. And at the centre is the still point to which I always return.

THE STILLEST DAY

The body which lay face down upon my bedroom floor still housed a possible life. A house from which all oxygen was perhaps now being expelled, one into which no light flowed through open eyes, occluded pupils. For the heart seemed to have discontinued its work. Those dependent on it were about to be destroyed.

My mother swayed a little and I feared for a moment that I might laugh. Two women, two mothers. One young and dead? The other old and dying? Then my mother looked at me with a strange and sudden coldness. And a thought came to me: had she ever loved me?

"Bethesda, we've only minutes. No more. Get me a knife."

"What?"

"Get me a knife. Do you have one here?"

"Yes. Yes, I do. My palette knife."

Suddenly I knew what she would do.

"Is it sharp?"

"Sharp? No."

"Then what? You must have something. Anything."

The mirror on which his face was painted lay hidden, wrapped in a silver-threaded shawl. This mirror refused to leave my conscious thought. It would trap me into action.

I stepped across the body of Mary Pearson and pulled open the bottom drawer of my bureau. I lifted the mirror which contained the first painting of his face, unwrapped it from its silver-threaded cloth, and smashed it. And then I smashed it further. Little of the image of Mathew Pearson's face remained intact.

My mother and I knelt beside the body of Mary Pearson and with difficulty turned the large animal-like thing over onto its back. She, whatever or whoever she had been, was gone. Departed.

We lifted her skirt which then fell over her face. Her body was corseted, vanity even *in extremis*. And for a moment something of her that was sweet moved me.

Then I concentrated all my will and all my strength to do my mother's bidding. I removed some of Mary Pearson's cotton underwear but, unable to undo the corset, I cut through the cloth – and then through part of her stomach. There was a sudden drenching red, shot through with light . . . impossible for the artist to capture. Then action blinded me to everything except the moment. And I cut deep. Remembering, as I cut, everything I had ever learned about human anatomy.

It was a fast and brutal journey. Down through tenacious forest of ligament and tissue, muscle and membrane. Until finally I reached the cavern of her womb, wet and dark, now unoxygenised and fetid. I removed the child. It was a girl. I handed her to my mother.

The pilgrimage of Mary Pearson's daughter from the womb to her first world, my room, had been fraught with difficulty. It had been perilous. And, like some grand adventure on a tumultuous sea, it was finally heroic and triumphant.

I pulled the skirt of Mary Pearson's dress over the open awfulness of her stomach and laid my silver-threaded shawl over her face. This cloth, in which the mirror image of her husband had lain, shaped itself, caul-like, over her features. Modesty was preserved. Horror was obscured. Mary Pearson, wife, was dead and Mary Pearson, mother, would never know her child.

A grotesque, magnificent still-life lay on my bedroom floor. And the image, as it seared itself on my mind, was not painted, nor even carved, but gouged, permanent and immutable, to be taken to the grave.

We cut the cord easily. And my mother's arthritic hands and mine, supposed to be those of the artist, had done the strangest thing. And no one cried. Not even for a time the baby. My mother turned the child face down and gently tapped it. The stillness was at an end.

The silence was at an end. For until that moment all had happened in a sorcery of silence and stillness.

I heard a knocking on the front door. I took the child from my mother. She refused to lean on me. And we descended. Two women and a female child. A moving tableau of power. Forward we glided towards the door. On the other side of which a man waited. My silver prince, this man who waited, unknowingly, for his life to shatter.

TWENTY-THREE

Paint two women in a doorway. Warrior women. Bloodied and triumphant as any man victorious upon the battlefield. One carries a child in her dripping arms. Paint a man transfixed.

Rest a while.

Paint a man as he follows a tracery of blood on a staircase which leads to an open door.

Rest a while.

Paint the face of a man as he absorbs the vision of a woman's body, blue-dressed, upon the floor. Paint, if you can, something of the individual onto the eternal, universal contours of grief.

Then attempt to paint the dark blood as it seeps and then seems to break over her.

Now paint the woman's face. It can be done. It has been done. Paint grey-white. Blue-white beneath shades of purple. Blonde curls, wet hieroglyphics, indecipherable on her forehead. Paint.

Rest a while.

Now paint a man carrying a body wrapped in bed linen. Walking, as though hypnotised, towards a visual cacophony of wailing women and whispering men.

Then rest.

And know that, later, sunset came down like a curtain. Know tomorrow did not wait. It did not hide in reverence or come a little late to show respect.

Know that bodies were washed. And know that rooms were hosed down. For the instinct to clean and to make new the site of agony is primitive. As someone, no doubt, washed the plates on which Titus Andronicus served to Queen Tamora the bodies of her children.

And thus in the village all was made appropriate on the night of the stillest day.

TWENTY-FOUR

The lust for normality is insatiable. And, because guidance is required, people turn to their age-old saviours, Church and State.

We gathered together in Lord Grantleigh's drawing room.

The Bishop was there. A necessary statement of hope in the spiritual.

And the headmaster was there. A necessary statement that lessons could be learned.

And the doctor was there. A necessary statement that the sick can be cured. And that, *in extremis*, someone has the authority to pronounce us dead.

All were seated. As was I, Bethesda Barnet. As was Mathew Pearson.

Lord Grantleigh stood, proprietorial, by his Elizabethan chimney-piece, as though protecting his inheritance. After the expression of his heartfelt condolences, he addressed himself to the subject of life, after the stillest day.

He told us of the doctor's confirmation of the instantaneous death of Mary Pearson from a fatal stroke.

And his statement was greeted with silence. Which is often believed to give assent.

He told us of the doctor's certainty that only the immediate and brave action of Miss Barnet and her mother had saved Mathew Pearson's daughter.

And again, no one spoke.

And then he told us with great emphasis of his absolute determination to protect the village which was in a ferment . . . a fever . . . a contagion . . .

I sat still. I sat so still as he spoke the words, "ferment", "fever", "contagion". I sat frozen in hushed immobility. An immobility in which even my breathing seemed stealthy, almost surreptitious.

I could paint a convocation of village faces expressive of expressionless questions as they gazed upon my own. And since even the inscrutable aspect of the human face has an awful eloquence, my silent painting would tell its tale. I had witnessed in the faces of those who had not witnessed the events of the stillest day a certain cryptic malignancy.

For there were other possible interpretations of what

had happened in my mother's house on that day. To those possible interpretations Lord Grantleigh made no reference. His silence and ours formed a wall against the avalanche which threatened to bury the temperate clemency in which our community had flourished.

Small societies practise best a democracy of silence. And sins of omission and commission fall softly into a collective, selective amnesia. For these societies know that they can bide their time. They know for they know the old stories: how the unacknowledged and therefore unpunished sin will in years to come be fully reckoned.

Finally, Lord Grantleigh quietly told us that in the fulfilment of our duty we would all find peace.

Still we listened to him without murmur, as though hypnotised. When it was over, we filed from Grantleigh Manor in a line, heads bowed and silent. It is a familiar painting, the slow procession of village inhabitants through a serenity of country scenery which implies tranquillity of soul. A timeless dissimulation.

I walked behind Mathew Pearson who did not wait for me. I walked behind Mathew Pearson who did not look at me, even as he opened his door and entered his house. His house, which in all of its dimensions, lines and proportions, was the very mirror of my own.

TWENTY-FIVE

That night as I lay in my bed which was placed against the wall, I heard the sound of gentle hammering. And then the sound of crumbling and a tiny aperture appeared in the common wall which separated my house from that of Mathew Pearson.

"Bethesda? Bethesda Barnet, can you hear me? Can your mother hear me?"

"My mother is sleeping, Mathew."

"And my Mary sleeps and my baby, who should have slept beside her mother, sleeps wet-nursed by a servant in the house of Alice Thomas."

"But you do not sleep, Mathew."

"And you do not sleep, Bethesda."

And then his hand . . . through the wall.

"Wrap your hair about my hand, Bethesda. Like a rope or a bandage."

THE STILLEST DAY

"Can you hear the pins tumble to the floor, Mathew?"

And I wrapped my hair, the colour of dull silver, round his hand. And felt the pain as he pulled it tight. I closed my eyes against it. I saw so clearly I could paint it a woman who did resemble me or who would be so identified were it necessary. And this woman lay prostrate on her bed joined by an urgency of hair to the ravenous hand which seemed to carve its way, greedy and yearning, through the wall.

This was the first infliction of pain. And I knew it would not be the last.

TWENTY-SIX

On the second night I lay on the cold floor, clothed. And with great speed wrapped my dull silver hair like a ribbon round his hand.

There was a reverberation of whispers in the dark room.

"Have I pulled your hair tight enough to make you weep, Bethesda?"

"You have, Mathew."

"Suffer it and listen to me."

I listened as he found in his confession absolution for his punishment of me. An old device.

I listened to him as he told me how when he first arrived in the village he believed he had made his way to a safe place. But instead had found me there.

I listened to him as he told me how he feared the world and always had.

I listened to him as he told me how he feared

women. Women who had always seen in him something that was not there. Women who were determined to capture it. Women who raged when they could not find what was never there.

And I listened to him as he told me that what he found with his wife, Mary, was comfort. Comfort and protection.

And I listened to him as he spoke of her. And I learned the old lesson of the unknowable heart of another. For he never spoke her name unless he preceded it with the words sweet, kind, gentle.

I listened to him as he told me that her fair curls gave light to her appearance. A light which spread throughout the gloom of his life after the death of his sister. I listened to him as he told how she blotted out the dark.

And I listened to him as he told me how she mourned when her parents died but had not raged against the world. How she did not throw sorrow like a mantle around her to keep out all joy. How she smiled steadily at life.

And I listened as he sang of the seasons of her goodness.

How in spring she relished spring.

How in summer her goldenness was at its most golden.

How autumn brought out in her another hue.

And how in winter she was quiet and content.

And, lest I did not understand, he told me how in every season her depths were no less deep because they were viewed through clear water.

And I listened to him as he told me that as a teacher of English he knew the list. And I listened as he told me how well he knew the stories.

I listened to him as he asked how many Cleopatras do we need to prove we can die for love? How many Othellos to prove we can kill for love? All the stories were the same, he said. Whomever one burns for, whether another's wife, sister, daughter or son, it was all heat. And the flames which burned would cool. And ashes were all that was left. Just ashes. And I listened to him as he told me that he had not burned for Mary. That he had loved her in all the purity of his heart.

And every line that he had ever read guided him as he wove his gentle, true-love hymn to Mary.

But he was not gentle as with a further tug he played upon my strung-out-tight-hair, the piercing scales of pain.

TWENTY-SEVEN

The third night after the stillest day. The night of Mary Pearson's funeral. The hand through the wall. And the voice, not whispering.

"I have been severed from myself, Bethesda. And now I will sever you from yourself. And I will break your life as you have broken mine."

"I know that, Mathew."

And I lay upon the cold floor, unclothed this time as he had requested. My hair tight-ribboned round his hand.

And I listened as he told me how he would hunt me down.

And I listened as he told me how he would lift my skirts in summer, and in winter.

And as I listened, images were painted on my mind of thorned roses and a haemorrhage of red petals, a summer gift. And of cold white candles which would light a fire in me, a winter gift.

And I listened, as though trapped in some echoic dream, to the future that he planned for me.

I would marry the noble Samuel Keans who had stood beside me so manfully after the stillest day. It would be a short-lived marriage. I would never have children.

He would marry Alice Thomas. And he would bring her to his house. And in time with Alice Thomas he would have more children.

I listened and shivered with pain and cold. And I knew that nothing about Mathew Pearson would ever be pure again.

TWENTY-EIGHT

As Mathew Pearson promised, these things did indeed come to pass. As they had an almost biblical force, I bowed my head in resignation.

Mathew Pearson married Alice Thomas. And everyone in the village forgave them. For their sudden marriage obliterated the horror of what had gone before. And the village rejoiced that people, like houses, could fold away old scenes of terror. Could roll them up like a discarded carpet and lay down another to walk upon.

I bowed my head in resignation as Mathew Pearson brought Alice Thomas to live with him in the house beside mine. I felt nothing. I heard the child cry at night. And I felt nothing. I heard other sounds, night after night. As I was meant to. And though I lay night after night beside the aperture, he did not come. I, Bethesda Barnet, endured it all. And I never wept.

After a short time, Samuel Keans prevailed. An act of

honour or defiance or maybe love. And he did not know that he prevailed according to Mathew Pearson's plan. Nor that it was in obedience to this plan that I married him.

And on my wedding night I went on a short, silent journey to a small inn in a nearby town.

A gift was waiting for us in our room. A box containing red roses and white candles. And in the box was a letter. It was from Mathew Pearson, addressed to my new husband.

In the morning Samuel Keans left me. He never returned to the village and his family. And I would imagine my name remains unblessed in their house.

And sick beyond shame, quietly I went home to live with my mother. To live again with her in the house beside Mathew Pearson, his wife Alice and his daughter, Mary.

And my only joy was to watch Alice Thomas as she grew to fear him.

And in those months the body of Alice Thomas seemed to follow some strange pattern and to grow fat then thin and then fat again as though she could find no shape to contain her grief.

TWENTY-NINE

"My God, Bethesda, you are a stupid woman. How could you have lost him? To wait all those years for Samuel Keans and to lose him in a night."

My mother's grief was wild and violent. And brought back memories of the wildness of her outbursts of long ago.

"I didn't lose him, Mother. He left."

"After a wedding night?"

"It would seem so."

"You needed him. You needed him like life itself. He rescued you."

"From what? I was not aware I had done anything wrong."

"I'm grateful to God, Bethesda, that He did not give me the eye of an artist. For what you don't see is truly terrifying. You seem not to see the subtle threads that bind us to our world here, the world in which we must make our lives. Fall through that net, Bethesda, and all your cleverness will be for nought.''

"I am on firm ground still, Mother. All will be well.''

"All will be well! And Alice Thomas now lives beside us. Mathew Pearson, supposedly deep in mourning for Mary – poor Mary – did not wait long.'' It was an old and bitter cry.

"No. But he had a child to consider.''

"Well, he could have considered it with you. He owes you so much, Bethesda. He owes you that child.''

"Us, Mother. He owes us.''

"Well, now you see, Bethesda, that life's great debts are rarely repaid. Alice Thomas has reaped a strange reward.''

And I thought how Alice Thomas had come to play a crucial part in my life. Alice Thomas, who for years I had considered to be a minor character in my story.

"All will be well, Mother.''

As I bowed my head again in resignation to these myriad blows, I thought my only remaining good fortune was to have as a patron such a man as Lord Grantleigh.

THIRTY

"Perhaps Tuesday as well as Thursday afternoons, Bethesda. Is that possible?"

"Certainly it is, Lord Grantleigh."

"Bethesda . . . how I love to speak your name after all those years of 'Miss Barnet'."

"And yet I continue to call you Lord Grantleigh."

"Perhaps more in deference to my age than for any other reason."

"Perhaps."

"You have changed, Bethesda. The gift of experience is a troublesome one."

"Yes, I am aware of that, Lord Grantleigh."

For I knew that my courage had been all used up. And though I had saved a life, a fact of which there was incontrovertible proof, I knew that the saving of a life is an ambivalent act. An act for which few are rewarded. Even those who have acted transparently can discern a note of hesitancy beneath the surface commendation. For perhaps one had interfered with the will of God? For God's infinite desire to remove us from this earth can never be doubted.

And at night, as I lay on the cold floor, my soul bereft and my hair unfettered, my eyes searched in every inch of cloth and wood and glass for my courage. But I could find no trace of it.

"Courage, Bethesda. *Courage, mon amie.*"

"I seem to have none left, Lord Grantleigh."

"It is a daily act of will, Bethesda."

"Then perhaps it is my will which burned in the furnace. I have none now. But have become rather fascinated to watch the will of others work in me."

"Mine, Bethesda?"

"Yours, Lord Grantleigh."

"And is your will nothing in this?"

"Other than in its acknowledgement of yours."

"You may be fatal to me, Bethesda. You stand here, your hair pinned tight against your head, magnificent, and talk of your defeat. A defeat which seems to have bred in you a languorousness that barely acknowledges what has happened between us. Your lack of will is your strength. Perhaps that is why images, long-trapped behind your artist's eye, now unshackled, float onto the canvas. You, who once painted elegant representations of church and school, now paint contorted female forms from which a sunflower sprouts while children seem to fall upon it hungry and you tell me that you see nothing. You tell me that your mother says you are blind and always have been. Where will I meet another such as you when I lose you, as I know I finally will?"

"A man like you, Lord Grantleigh, loses little."

"I bow more often than you might imagine, my dear."

"Not to me, Lord Grantleigh."

"You have no need of it, Bethesda. You have me body and soul."

"Not heart, Lord Grantleigh?"

"The heart is a poor thing, Bethesda."

"It still rests with 'the fiend'?"

"Perhaps. How far we have come, you and I, Bethesda. I fear that our honesty has a quality of finality about it. When there is nothing to preserve, only then are men and women honest with each other."

I realised, as I walked home that day, that I had been warned. And I knew that should another blow fall, I would surrender myself to it. I would withdraw into solitude and silence. For perhaps, in truth, my life's work was done.

THIRTY-ONE

The letter read:

My Dear Bethesda,

A precarious position can be held for a lifetime. What is required is the recognition of vulnerability and an almost artistic feel for the subtle balance of the thing. When that is lost, the inherent weakness of the structure precipitates an immediate collapse.

I can no longer be your protector. Forgive me. I may have to watch you fall without a murmur. But though dishonourable, I am not a villain. I will use my power to find a refuge for you. But elsewhere. Outside my kingdom which your presence has threatened. I underestimated the damage I would suffer in my protection of you after Mary Pearson's death. I may have quelled the questions and fears

*of the village but they remain purling under the surface. A
fact, no doubt, of which you are aware.*

*And Samuel Keans made a fateful comment in his
precipitative desertion of you. The village does not dare to
guess what it was he found. It is best not to know. But
clearly, Bethesda, it was not wholesome to him.*

*Lady Grantleigh has informed me, Bethesda, that your
position is untenable. Her words were, as ever, to the
point.*

*"You were her saviour and her protector, sir. To that I
could accommodate myself. But you were not content with
that. Remove her from this village. And do so quickly."*

*Perhaps you will even smile, Bethesda, when I tell you
the response of the various people I visited in order to
investigate the possibilities of a new life for you and your
mother.*

*The Bishop said: "I know a place. It is run by a
contemplative order. Miss Barnet has once or twice
remarked to one of the younger priests that she had
considered withdrawal from the world. Her mother, of
course, remains a problem."*

*Nurse Ryder at the cottage hospital vouchsafed: "A
room in the hospital? A permanent room for Mrs Barnet?
But we don't have a free room at the moment, Lord
Grantleigh . . . I see you are determined . . . Yes, I am*

conscious of all you have done for us. But are you aware, Lord Grantleigh, that we have long wished for an extension to house sick children. An annexe away from the adults whose behaviour in their last illness is not always exemplary?"

"Ah, indeed, Nurse Ryder." I replied. "Suffer the little children. It's quite extraordinary but such an extension has long been on my mind."

There is another possibility, Bethesda. I will simply state that it exists. It would dishonour us both to press the matter.

The Managing Agent, Wimpole Mansions in London, said: "A suite of rooms, Lord Grantleigh? For your own use? No? I see. I'm sure that can be arranged. The name of the young lady. . . ?"

The choice is yours, Bethesda. In a sense, I have none.

Bethesda, I am trapped. And I am a man who cannot remain trapped for long. To use a common parlance, "the game is up". My Irish hound has triumphed. The fiend is unforgiving. Relentless. And she has hostages. My children. I must obey. Medea never rode her chariot with as much raging abandonment as my fiend now rides to the kill.

After she found me with you, she laughed. "I've got you both at last." And indeed, Bethesda, so she had.

THE STILLEST DAY

Neither of us must ever forget that families like mine are dynastic. My present life simply feeds the river. That I should make you leave, alas, convinces me that I am a lesser man than I had previously believed.

But I must cleave you from me. Your clever face. Your new paintings which begin to haunt me. I have a feeling, Bethesda, perhaps even a fear, that I am separating myself from you at the very moment at which you may be about to become extraordinary.

I tell you, Bethesda Barnet, I am not so foolish as to be unaware that you were the most glorious thing in my life. But my life was never my own. Please remember I am not an important battle for you.

I know that we will have no difficult meetings. You will make your decision without tears or supplication. I have been your lover and would wish to remain so. But elsewhere, Bethesda. From now on, elsewhere.

It is a measure of my deep faith in you that I should write you such a letter.

I love, worship and adore you, Bethesda Barnet. But, of course, as so often, that is not enough. Forgive me.

I am,

Ever yours,

Edgar Grantleigh.

And so my life was organised out of the picture, as lives often are. Weary, I acquiesced. For the exhausted need a master. And in his own way, Lord Grantleigh was benign.

My mother accepted the price of her survival. For she and I both knew that the quiet, unmarked years of that side-by-side life we had lived together had been lost in a tumult of action. The simple, straight road which we had trod day after day in an eternity of hours had led to a precipice.

And, though we had not fallen, we could not turn back. The road was blocked by the isolation of an experience none could share. She would be housed like some wounded bird in the least treacherous curve of the cliff. And she would have to watch while I walked along the edge down a different path. I would not look back and she would not wave. For the simple reason that neither of us could. All our attention must now be concentrated on the careful and restrained extension of our remaining time on earth.

We had both been smashed and recast not in bronze or plaster but in the iron containment of the will.

Time, after the extreme moment, is for contemplation only. Those who survive the journey to the edge or those who have been in the abyss do not live on borrowed time. They live on stolen time. And wish, perhaps, to return it unused, unsullied and unlived.

THIRTY-TWO

The island, when I first saw it, seemed to me an orb of the most profound bleakness. Desolate, it lay encircled by the cold, reflecting movement of the mirrored surface of the lake. As though the water held it in an aloof and frosty embrace. Ringed by cypress trees: these deferential guardians almost obscured a grey masonry of Gothic imperfection.

I had travelled from a world where the very stones had been carved into shapes of adoration, to another self-same world. A circular journey leading to the first place. And it seemed that the place had been designed for what I had become.

I needed another fortress. My mother had found hers. And as I set out for mine I hoped that perhaps this time, in strict adherence to its rules and ritual, I could withdraw entirely into silence and solitude.

It was a place to hide me, now that I had become a

thing to be hidden. It was a place of silence, now that I had imposed silence upon myself. Perhaps I knew when I arrived that I had waited in life for too long.

Feverish with inactivity, I had acted with wild precision for a single hour. On this island, I knew my exhausted soul would fall back upon itself. To wait again . . .

THIRTY-THREE

" She has been absolved from her vow of silence. For the purpose of your visit. This is her door. Locked, of course. Sit down here, sir, on this bench. Note the inscription . . . *De necessitátibus meis éripe me, Dómine.* Normally, sir, the cloisters are bare of seating but I had to insist that a bench be placed here, just outside her rooms. Because, frankly, there have been times when I have been so weakened by encounters with her that I have had to sit and rest before I could undertake the tortuous journey back to the refectory. If we wait here, sir, Reverend Mother will join us shortly."

I listened silently in my room to Doctor Peder Strauss. A man, not old, who had chosen some years ago and for perhaps dubious reasons to exile himself to a small town on the edge of a lake in what was to him a foreign country. And there, in a wilful waste of his training, to become the visiting doctor to our island convent.

And I, who knew of apertures and deception, of the design of delusion and of sounds through walls, of the permeability of what we once thought impermeable, had for many years watched him covertly as he sat, head in hands, outside my room. His sighs and exhausted mutterings to the unresponsive silence of the empty cloisters had never elicited pity from me.

Now a companion sat beside him. In lust for communication Doctor Strauss raced to language. And I overheard the things that I already knew. As illicit listeners usually do.

"This building is daunting, sir. Endless corridors, steps, staircases leading where, I sometimes wonder? Took me years to work it out. The crossing must have been appalling, sir. Such a short journey and yet often so turbulent. I've been trapped here once or twice sometimes for up to two or three days in winter. Particularly in February. Not something I relish, I can tell you. The delicacy with which one must approach them, the possibility for misinterpretation. The endless, endless possibility for misinterpretation. Even one visit is enough to leave me feeling quite, quite depleted. I remember that surprised me at the beginning. Shocked

me even. Does it not shock you? I expected to feel
refreshed, even nourished. I rarely talk about this with
my family. I am not certain whose will prevails. Mine or
theirs. Who decided silence was best? Even my male
friends, even the coarsest, say little really. Oh, the odd
lewd remark, the occasional slightly prurient question,
but on the whole fewer than I had feared.

"My wife? Well, so much happens in the dark in
marriage. I speak metaphorically, of course. I do not
wish you to think me indelicate in any way. My
daughter? Fathers and daughters, it's such a complicated
and dangerous − yes, yes − I really mean dangerous
relationship. I am so careful. I cannot begin to tell you
how fastidious I am.

"But my son envies me, I suppose. He is young but
cursed as we men are so early with imagination. Is that
the right word? Imagination, images, imagery in these
matters. That I should know the answers, well at least
the most obvious answers, is difficult for him. My
knowledge is so specific, so physical. A medical
knowledge. Permitted access, privileged access to the
female form. Forgive me. I don't wish to embarrass you.
But if I said anything to him it would only make matters
worse. I mean, how could I, his father, endeavour to
teach him? Well, that has been my decision anyway. Say

nothing. My own father was the same. It's more dignified, don't you think? I find the garrulous vulgar, don't you? Uncouth. That was my father's word. Uncouth. He rhymed it with youth when he wanted to, to what . . . ? Chastise me? That was his word too. Chastise. I always thought of chaste. The word chaste when he said chastise.

"So, it's been my decision never to use those words to my son. Don't want to start up the same cacophony. I got that word from my wife. And the music, of course. She's a musician. She plays piano. Her fingers are so strong. So flexible, supple. I watch her fingers racing up and down the keyboard and . . . do you know something? I hardly hear the music. I'm so absorbed by her hands. Astonishing. I feel privileged just to watch her. Just to watch her fingers on the keyboard. I used to believe before I met her that musicians had long, elegant fingers. But it's not true. Well, of course, maybe some do but my wife's fingers are strong. Elegant and strong and not long. Well, not especially long. She creates states of ecstasy. For herself. For me. For others. Just with her fingers on the keyboards. I envy her. Do you know that? I envy my wife . . ."

Like a symbolic cymbal, her crucifix as it fell against the keys about her waist heralded the approach of

Reverend Mother and the sudden silence of Doctor Strauss.

The clank of wood on metal combined with the whispering swish of her skirts on the stone floor should have warned but more often hypnotised the listener. Sisters engaged in some minor infringement of their Order's orders surrendered when escape would in fact have been possible. We permit authority. And the rustle of rules as we brush against them creates the illusion of a silken cradle.

"Good evening, sir. Forgive me that I was not there to greet you when you arrived. Doctor Strauss and I thought it best that you should first see her sleeping. The features are less . . ."

"Distorted."

"Yes, that's the word. Thank you, Doctor Strauss. Ah, here is the key . . . I know you must be cold and hungry, sir, but I thought you'd want to see her immediately. Just to look at her. Well. . . ? Well, sir? Sir. . . ? *Sir?*"

THIRTY-FOUR

And there is nothing easier to feign than sleep. And since, even in sleep, I had a look about me . . .

And as they left my room I heard the metalline sound of the key in the lock. And after metal on metal came silence. And then words, again. I let their words wash over me. An ablution without absolution.

"We should have warned you, sir. Doctor Strauss and I are, of course, no longer shocked. But for you . . ."

"Sit down, sir. You are very pale. Rest here for a moment. I'll bring some water from Sister Jacinta's room. It's just down the corridor. Perhaps then, Reverend Mother, with your permission we can proceed to supper?"

"Thank you, Doctor Strauss. Should I ask our guest to incline his head, Doctor Strauss, does that help?"

Ah, minister to him, Reverend Mother. Do not let

him slip away. But who has power to keep him? Not Doctor Strauss, who tries as ever to soothe . . .

"Please don't worry, Reverend Mother. It is nothing serious. I'll get the water."

And as he hurries down the convent corridor, she hurries down a corridor of words. Each of them madly purposeful to no purpose.

". . . Oh dear. You must have found the long corridors daunting and cold, sir. Particularly the colonnades, sections of which are open to the elements. No doubt the architect of the building was driven by the spiritual possibilities inherent in such an undertaking. Perhaps God guided him to the knowledge that a long, cold and bitter walk from chapel to dining room increased the opportunity for the mortification of the appetite. So that when the Sisters finally arrive in the dining room they are profoundly grateful to God for their meal.

"Certain members of our Order enter such states of ecstasy in their gratitude to The Lord, for having provided them with the opportunity for mortification of appetite, that on arrival at table they cannot eat at all. They simply refuse to desist from the ecstasy of their hunger. Nor from the ecstasy which follows the annihilation of the self and its appetites. Do I talk too much, sir? Ah, thank you, Doctor Strauss. Drink this, sir.''

"We are often ambushed by words, Reverend Mother. Particularly when we speak here in a house of silence.''

"Yes, Doctor Strauss, speech after silence can be exhausting for both speaker and listener. I have been wholly absolved from my own vow of silence for the period of your visit. As has Sister Jacinta who will cook and minister to us. I ask myself is this absolution a blessing? The moment I start to speak, the words seem to consume me. To almost devour me. How do you think he looks now, Doctor Strauss?''

"Better. Much, much better, Reverend Mother. If we just wait here quietly for a few more minutes . . .''

"A little more water, sir? We are so grateful to you for coming. And so grateful to our patron for sending you. Doctor Strauss and I hesitated a great deal before contacting him on this matter. Finally we decided it was essential. We felt we had to act when one of the lay sisters described a painting to us. Sister Virginia had only glimpsed it for a second as it was being moved into the workroom. But what Sister Virginia described . . .''

And what eye did Sister Virginia bring to my paintings? An eye which had gazed on nothing other than convent walls. Unjust of me to judge her so. I, whose whole life changed in a second's vision of a rain-drenched face. I, who had been transfixed by the vision of an eye and had almost felt the perverse caress of a leopard, golden-haired, with the creamy face of a sphinx.

". . . to the best of my knowledge, sir, no one other than Sister Virginia has ever seen the paintings . . ."

"That is correct, Reverend Mother. Even I, her doctor, who has so often been called to her room after various . . . incidents, have never managed to catch even a glimpse . . . in fact I sometimes wonder, do they exist at all?"

"Her patron, our patron, insisted that there should be only one key to her workroom. And she hides this key about her person. So many concessions to this Sister. Too many, I say, Doctor Strauss."

"Perhaps, Reverend Mother."

"From the beginning, our patron was most insistent. We were compelled by him to allow her to do what she wished in this matter. Everything to do with her painting has been supported, indeed financed, by him. It was a condition of his continued patronage of the convent that every facility must be made available to her. What Doctor Strauss has just referred to as her workroom is a specially adapted studio much resented by the other

Sisters. And she is also exempted from certain duties. Oh, I can't tell you, the list is endless. Endless concessions.''

"Reverend Mother is correct. There are many concessions to this Sister."

"However, we must obey since our patron is so beneficent."

"As he is to me. After all, I am only a humble doctor."

"Come now, Doctor Strauss. We know of your many qualifications. How many country doctors have had your experience? Particularly in Europe? It was our patron who first directed you here. You met him in Paris, did you not?"

"Yes, Reverend Mother. During a particularly . . . difficult time in my life."

"Please don't misunderstand us, sir. Our Order is eternally grateful to our patron for his generosity. With the arrival of Sister Annunciata, which at the time we had no idea was going to cause such difficulty, he gave this island to the Order as an outright gift. Prior to that we paid an annual rent out of other small endowments. Major renovations also paid for by our patron were undertaken. The castle, our nunnery was in very poor repair."

"You can see, sir, that the Reverend Mother and I are anxious both to obey and protect him in this matter."

"Doctor Strauss is aware, sir, that it is my responsibility too, to protect the Order. We need new postulants all the time and any scandal could affect us. Families might be reluctant to allow their daughters to enter the Order . . ."

"Sir, the letter Reverend Mother and I wrote to our patron has, I know, been made available to you. I gather it was after much reflection that he decided you were the person best able to deal discreetly with this matter. The situation is difficult to clarify. It is our hope that you fully comprehend our dilemma. We were informed last week that we should expect a visit from a gentleman, either this Sunday or next. I'm afraid he did not give us your name."

"Doctor Strauss and I believe that we should act urgently. I have of course on more than one occasion intimated to her that complete dispensation from her vows could be arranged. She resisted this. Passionately. 'I will not leave,' was all she would say. 'I am waiting.' Isn't that correct, Doctor Strauss?"

"Indeed, Reverend Mother. Our difficulty, sir, is that rumours are now spreading from the island to the mainland. The whole thing could quite quickly become intolerable.''

"And do remember, sir, not all my Sisters have taken a full vow of silence. The junior lay nuns, for example. They are prohibited of course from chatter. Chitter-chattering, I call it. I feel one of them may have whispered a story, a fantasy, to an outsider . . .''

"Look, Reverend Mother. His colour has returned. Shall we proceed to the refectory? Would you care to take my arm, sir?''

"Let us go immediately to the refectory, sir. You will be pleased to hear, Doctor Strauss, that we have prepared your favourite soup, celery soup, creamed. It is a difficult decision whether to bite into the white castellation of the celery stalk and to reduce it with one's teeth to another consistency, or to allow Sister Jacinta to soften it and then pound it and then cream it. We shall have wine, because of your slight indisposition, sir. Other than medicinally, wine is very rarely served. However, since we daily eat and drink the body and blood of Our Lord we are not lacking in sustenance. Come with us, sir, and we will nourish you . . .''

And the echo, not unpleasing, of her crucifix as it struck upon the keys, betokened her departure as it had earlier augured her arrival. And the corridor outside my room was shrouded in silence again as the sound of their footsteps, his indecipherable from those of Reverend Mother and Doctor Strauss, ebbed away and was finally lost to me.

THIRTY-FIVE

The habit of habit, irrespective of habitation . . . The hours of the night . . . hours unslept painting a vision of a vision from memory which is all vision.

For many years here my daily life had followed the same pattern. And did so this morning. I rose at six-thirty and bathed meticulously, monotonously, as though the water which flowed over my body obeyed the rhythm of the tides.

Then I robed myself in another habit. And, today as on all others, I waited . . . And waiting can become an ecstasy of abstinence. Fuelled by the absolute power of will.

. . . Eventually, and as ever, if one stands quite still in a state of perpetual purposeful abandonment of all other desires, the moment for which one has waited, arrives. And, as ever, it too passes.

I had stood rooted like one of the cypress trees which

surrounded my consecrated domain. Like them, I had
borne the heat in summer and the heavy snow in winter
without murmur or complaint.

And since within my cloistered world silence was not
only an imperative but my secret succour, I had stood an
immutable testament to powerful passivity. A power
which gathers from the air around it all its energy and
holds it soundlessly in the fathomless well of the soul. A
power which, though silent, somehow reverberates down
long, secret corridors of airy sky until the person whose
name we have but breathed turns suddenly, helplessly,
towards us.

It is irrelevant that some other force may be deemed
the catalyst. Those who have waited down the years of
time know that predatory patience will always triumph.

With passionless passion I had pushed myself to an
extreme. And when that extreme proved itself futile, I
had pushed further.

As always, those forced to watch a trembling ballet at
the edge of madness believe themselves obliged to act.
For is it not sacred duty which compels one human
being, though unbidden, to attempt another's salvation?
The agents of coercion, caritas, fear or self-preservation,
have an ancient potency. So that in a maze of
misunderstanding lost souls are pulled back from the

path which they were destined to follow. Now aware of the necessity of cunning, they appear to succumb to this unwelcome care. And all the while, patiently, stoically, they bide their time until another route to their elected exit presents itself to their ever-watchful, unfaltering eye.

After what was perhaps an hour of contemplation I left my chair and lay on my bed. When seated I felt that the angle at which a sudden ray of morning light fell on my face highlighted the slight distortion of my eyelid. I had carefully created this effect some months ago with Doctor Strauss's unintentional help. He has an almost obsessive desire to sew up even superficial wounds. Though mirrors are banned it is still possible to glimpse oneself in water – hydromancy. Or in windows, wine and blood – cryptallomancy.

I recognised myself more easily when the vision that returned to me bore his resemblance. The identification of oneself is a conundrum. Proved in the mirror more often than in the eye of another?

And finally, this morning warned by the familiar sound of crucifix on keys . . .

And now the selected key in the lock . . .

And then . . .

"Good morning, Sister Annunciata."

She does not expect a reply.

She chooses as always to sit in a position in which she is exposed as little as possible to a sight she abhors. We both wait.

And then . . .

"Good morning, Doctor Strauss."

"Good morning, Reverend Mother. Sister Annunciata . . ."

He expects no reply.

And into the silence falls Reverend Mother's voice:

"I have sent Sister Jacinta to collect our visitor. He should be here shortly, Doctor Strauss."

Silence, followed by footfalls. Followed by the echo of footfalls. Another person enters the room. One who elects to stand in an adumbration of winter-morning shadows. Adding to them, densifying them. And I call into the shadows.

An old silence is shattered. Not just the silent years which have been broken only in delirium during Doctor Strauss' agitated visits. But another, deeper silence. A silence in which language, unspoken, has become weighted with dreams. Each word has sunk beneath a baroque embroidery of memory and hope, to lie unused in the depths of my mind. Now an obscure force, a tenebrous eidolon, disengages them from their resting place. I think I see them float, smoky-pale amorphous shapes, to the surface, streaming their undulating, delicate tracery.

"You . . . yes, you in the shadow . . ."

And though I speak softly, I sense in the shocking reverberation of sound other words, disturbed and trembling, assemble as though for an assault on both myself and the listeners.

Silence.

"Reverend Mother, Doctor Strauss, who permitted access to this person?"

Silence.

"Sir, who permitted you access? I have certain rights here, certain privileges. Speak, sir."

Silence.

"What? No word. No word from the shadows? Perhaps I know you. You must forgive me that I do not rise to greet you. I'm lying down because the weight of my life is so heavy. It presses on me. It crushes me. And I was asked to carry this weight alone. Finally, even my mother could not help me. Poor mother.

"I have a question for you, sir. Do I, Bethesda Barnet, lie here beneath a weight of shame? Shame which bundled itself up and fell upon me like old, soiled, heavy bed linen. Or am I Bethesda Barnet who collapsed under the weight of her history which quite stole her away? Or does nothing bear down on me at all? God has not yet answered these questions for me. Perhaps you can, sir.''

But I know he can't. What makes us always hope that the shadow has substance? He cannot tell me whether I am lying here a white and black geometry on the green coverlet in this stone-grey room because all my life's energies were expended in one moment. A moment which mastered me. A moment which pressed my soul as though through a mangle and flattened it. And beat it down to nothing.

Reverend Mother sits motionless and that her calm is uncelestial can be discerned in the raging of her eyes. Doctor Strauss, head bowed, makes of his fingers a Gothic structure against which his forehead rests. And from the dark morning shadows I can discern nothing. I wonder about the story which brought us all here. And about how, in time, it will be told.

And I call to the shadows again.

''I knew I should expect a visitor. Were you the one who came last night, sir? Were you the one who thought I was sleeping? Dreaming, perhaps. But I sensed a presence. I'm never wrong in these matters. This morning I rose early, bathed and dressed. I followed all my old rituals. Which I quickly discovered years ago were even more austere than those practised here. At least in relation to my ablutions. Is that acceptable to you — that word? Is it delicate enough? It's not that I worship delicacy of feeling or expression to the exclusion of all else. As I have proved, I can be brutal. When brutality is required. So many people can't. They don't understand the essential nature of brutality. That it is, so often, essential. Do you agree, sir, that brutality is often essential? Your silence, sir, is a conceit . . . Answer me, sir. Is brutality essential? Was it essential?

"Do you know what I'm called now, sir? Sister Annunciata. A name which celebrates The Annunciation. As the name Mary always celebrates the divine nature of motherhood. Even to those who do not give birth to a god. Why do we always celebrate the annunciation of a birth to come? Perhaps she, Mary, the first Mary, chosen to be the Mother of God, was not happy to have been so chosen. After all, it was such a heavy burden in every way. And we are never told whether it was an easy pregnancy or not. Perhaps it's best not to know. It was, of course, impossible for her to refuse The Holy Ghost, The Shadow. 'And The Shadow came over her'. Is that not what we are taught? What if she had said, 'Take this child to another womb, there's no room here'? Was she tempted to say that, I wonder? But then, once the child was in the womb she was trapped. So was the child.

One forgets that. That living entombment with no way out. At least for months. Is there a warning to the child? Exile awaits you. The silence and solitude will end . . . And then we know so little about the birth. Though one must assume it was natural. Not helped in any way. There is, I believe, sir, no reference in The Bible to instruments . . ."

"*Sister Annunciata!*"

Reverend Mother, almost screaming, scatters the remnants of her serenity around the room.

"This is sacrilege! Sacrilege, I tell you! I absolutely forbid you to continue with this. I am patient. I am endlessly patient as you endeavour to destroy the sacred, solemn foundations of this Order. Doctor Strauss, it is surely not beyond your abilities to give something, anything, to this Sister to stop her . . ."

"Calm yourself, Reverend Mother. Forgive me speaking to you like this, but we have so little time. Our guest will leave tomorrow. He is most insistent. As is our patron. Sister Annunciata has never been as strict in her adherence to the rules of silence as the other Sisters. Some of these comments I have heard from her before."

"Well, I have *not*, Doctor Strauss. I *insist* that you give her something to calm her. Even for a short time.

THE STILLEST DAY

Sir, I would like to talk to you outside this room. Please follow me."

And as one man leaves, another approaches, bottle in hand.

"Doctor Strauss," I whisper, "I have a gift for you, Doctor Strauss. A single, perfect finger. Small, the little finger. And it is cut right through to the bone. A perfect painting. Small, but perfect, like the finger. You shall have it later. Put the bottle away, Doctor Strauss, and you shall have the painting. Otherwise I will destroy it."

Art is a dream behind the eyes. And not only for the artist. And the imagined unimaginable is always recognised as it swoons onto canvas in a faint of colour. Sighing, Doctor Strauss takes my offering. Poor Doctor Strauss, condemned to work with the flesh and the mind when the great love of his life is bone. For that is what the artist in him worships. Particularly the finger bones of his wife, the pianist. Why, I wonder as he leaves the room, has he not pursued the life of a surgeon. . . ?

Alone again, I close my eyes and create a painting of an artist with steel-tipped brushes exquisitely, assiduously searching and exposing in the human body the beauty of the bone.

Absorbed in this vision of the unfolding skeleton, I allow Reverend Mother's disembodied voice, once vestal, to drift in and out of my mind as she paces the cloisters outside my room and rages against "the loathsome Bethesda Barnet" . . .

THIRTY-SIX

". . . *Yes!* She is loathsome . . . Forgive me, sir, forgive me, Doctor Strauss, I do not normally speak so frankly. She is an aberration. She thinks herself an artist. I loathe the artist. I mean the creative artist, of course, Doctor Strauss. Your wife is an interpretative artist, interprets brilliantly the work of others. Like the actor. Generous souls searching in themselves for ways to serve. But the creative artist, that vulture swooping down on life, searching with its cruel eye for a way to recreate the world, is ungodly. Yes, they *are* ungodly. I will go further. They are *against* God. The very person most interpretative artists believe they serve. Just tell me, Doctor Strauss, has any artist ever been canonised? I am aware, of course, Doctor Strauss, that your wife is a kind of saint."

"She is indeed, Reverend Mother, a very saintly woman. And an artist."

"Bethesda Barnet may believe herself to be an artist but she is not a saintly woman. In fact, she is my most troublesome Sister. She is my most *ungodly* Sister. And I use the word ungodly, deliberately. The loathsome Sister Annunciata! Though I'm afraid I no longer think of her in that guise. Was it always a guise perhaps? On the other hand, maybe God did call her. Maybe she heard Him correctly. What a terrible thought. Is it possible, Doctor Strauss, that Bethesda Barnet could have heard Him correctly?"

"It is a great mystery to the layman like myself, Reverend Mother, that the call is silent. How difficult therefore to be certain one has interpreted it correctly. Interpretation is all. Whether of speech or silence."

"You put it so elegantly, Doctor Strauss. Do you think our guest has correctly interpreted our dilemma?"

"And even more important, Reverend Mother, will he find a solution for us? A way out, so to speak."

"We do not wish to press you, sir. Please do not believe we are ungrateful to you for coming here at such a difficult time of the year. The snow, the storms. Oh forgive me, sir, did you sleep last night . . . through the storm. . . ?"

THE STILLEST DAY

I feel certain he did not sleep last night. And not only because of the storm. Which was severe. As behoves a storm. Though the eye is always calm, they say. It's a disturbing image. Is it beyond me to catch the eye of the storm and trap it, somewhere on my canvas? Which painting should contain, perhaps in the shadows, the eye of the storm? Which one should contain the vortex, spiralling in its perfect helix and at its centre the void? That perfect nothingness. Into which Doctor Strauss's voice now falls . . .

". . . Anyway you came. I thank God for that. Sir, I hope that from this conversation you begin to discern the outline of a plan. Is that possible, sir? That you have a plan?"

"Doctor Strauss and I hope that we have not been obtuse, sir. When one is unused to speech it rather takes one by surprise. The words explode from their prison in a sense, or not in a sense, I fear. They are not correctly arranged perhaps. Do you think we have correctly arranged the words, Doctor Strauss?"

"Perhaps, Reverend Mother, what we need for our visitor is notation. In order to discern the shape of the thing. Is it a sonata, I ask myself? Is that the shape? Or a fugue? I wish, oh how I wish, I could discuss this with my wife. Give her the sounds and let her arrange them.''

"Let us be frank with our guest, Doctor Strauss. Bethesda Barnet may be, indeed *is*, an hysteric. A dangerous one. Dangerous to herself. Dangerous to us. Dangerous to our patron. What does our guest think? You are very discreet, sir.''

"Or perhaps our guest is exhausted. We have had a difficult day, Reverend Mother. Certain fragments of Sister Annunciata's conversation seemed almost to fly like gunshot, around the room. One felt one might be wounded. Frankly, Reverend Mother, I feared she might attack us. Ridiculous, I know, when she is so weak. She has disturbed us. She has seriously disturbed us all, sir.''

"Doctor Strauss is right. And yet Sister Annunciata seemed well enough when she first arrived here. We knew that something strange had happened. Our patron implied certain difficulties but as I explained to you in many ways we saw her as a blessing. Indeed, that year I saw her as a kind of salvation for our Order. And we all have our secrets. I felt that in the silence of a convent, no questions . . . an absence of accusation. Our examination of conscience is silent. And whatever she had to confess I felt certain she must have confessed before she came here. God is ever merciful. And our patron was generous. And in that perfect combination of charity I welcomed Bethesda Barnet. She was a little sorrowful of course but I put that down to leaving her mother. She was an only child and much attached to her mother.''

''. . . who died last month, sir.''

''Indeed, Doctor Strauss. I myself had to call her from prayers and tell her the news.''

''She took it calmly, I believe, Reverend Mother.''

''Very calmly, Doctor Strauss. Perhaps *too* calmly. She did not even weep when I reiterated the rules concerning funerals. That we are not allowed to leave the convent even for the burial of our nearest relatives. It is a test of faith. After all, we will see them in the next life. She just bowed her head, which surprised me. And it was the last parent . . . her father had died years before. But then I find one mourns one or other parent, rarely both. And one always mourns the one least loved.''

''One of life's mysteries, Reverend Mother?''

''We must respect mysteries, Doctor Strauss. Indeed, I would go further — an unquestioning acceptance of mystery is essential in spiritual life. I believe mystery should *never* be investigated. Medicine has its mysteries too, Doctor Strauss, would you not agree?''

"We so rarely disagree, Reverend Mother. However, a doctor's job must be to investigate the mysteries of the body. To discover the source of the pain."

"Yet you of all people know, Doctor Strauss, that we die as frequently from painless ailments as from physical agony. My father, for example – the parent much missed though least loved – he had no pain at all. He just died, suddenly, one day."

"So much happens suddenly, Reverend Mother. Our guest, for example, suddenly, he is here. And suddenly, perhaps in hours, he will leave and . . . suddenly, all will be back to normal. A sudden normality. Not what we expect, is it?"

"You're right, Doctor Strauss. And yet sometimes there it is. Suddenly. Normality. God-given. A reward for having stepped back from the abyss. The abyss, Doctor Strauss, in which you once told me truth was to be found. Do you still believe that, Doctor Strauss? Is truth found in the abyss?"

"If it is, Reverend Mother, the question surely is, if truth lies there are we compelled to descend, however precipitous the journey?"

"How much more appealing, Doctor Strauss, to believe, in gazing upwards towards the light, that truth lies there."

THE STILLEST DAY

"Both descent and ascent are dangerous, Reverend Mother. Indeed, perhaps we are caught *au juste milieu*. A phrase Sister Annunciata once used to describe certain aspects of painting. I think it was after the last incident when it was necessary to give her certain substances . . . to alleviate the pain."

"*Juste milieu*, Doctor Strauss?"

"Between truth and lies, Reverend Mother. Between love and hate. Between good and evil. An eternal, essential oscillation."

"Are you implying, Doctor, that the safest place is the *juste milieu*?"

"Well, if it is, Reverend Mother, I suspect that it is not where the soul of Sister Annunciata lies."

THIRTY-SEVEN

Dear Doctor Strauss. Poor Doctor Strauss. The essence of whose being is hidden deep in the finger bones of his wife. Blind to his own obsession as he is deaf to his wife's music, he yet believes he can locate my soul.

If he could but look at me with the eye of an artist which, of course, he does not have, he would see that I am a study, an *étude* in three forms of possession, that of mind, that of soul, that of body. A perfect, living self-portrait. In exquisite pieces. And it is in reflection that they float together to form a whole. Sometimes, reflected in water, I can see someone else behind me. Just a face. The face of a woman. I never see the face of the child.

I need to see myself. I must be sure that it is Bethesda Barnet they see. It is essential that I get a mirror. I must persuade Reverend Mother to let me have a mirror. It is the one rule about which she is perpetually adamant. I must find a way.

Perhaps they fear what I will see in the mirror. Perhaps I will see that I am now my mother. My mother when she walked upright. And this facial distortion which I feel? It's nothing. Nothing. When I touch the scar, my fingertips tell the story of tautened skin above muscle, which has been slightly wrenched from its normal position. An artist would be praised for this original reshaping of the physiognomy. Someone will smash the face and gather it up differently some day. And Doctor Strauss's little stitches are perhaps pretty. Yes, I feel certain that he sews pretty little stitches. Has it occurred to him, I wonder, that they form a keyboard on my neck?

My mother's dead now. Naturally. She died old and naturally. When she was young, she tried to kill herself. Eyes closed, she whispered a confession to me on the day we parted: for which I was not sanctioned to give absolution. Once I told her story to Doctor Strauss. I told him how, while she lay bleeding, dying for love, she had been violated by the doctor who came to save her.

Yet Doctor Strauss felt no desire for me when he found me bleeding. I laid myself open to him and he refused me. I often think of the two cuts, neck and abdomen . . . I could paint the cuts to the same design. Twinned cicatrices.

We commit the same sins as our parents. It is an act of love. To show we understand. To show that we are one with them. It's an instinct which has its own artistic imperative. So this distortion is nothing. I lived, as she did. But childless. Though I brought another into the world, yet I'm childless.

Marauding memory. Raging and ravaging. I cannot stop. I cannot stop.

I gave no one the broken mirror. Though it disappeared that day. I often think on that. But then what is broken can't heal us. We need the illusion that things will not break and crack and suck us under. We need gifts which are whole. Dismemberment, distortion, desecration all disturb us.

I remember that there was a mirror from China . . . in a large room just off a conservatory. The mirror was black with scarlet fans, like skirts, painted on it. And strange, predatory birds. Perhaps Lord Grantleigh found some aspect of himself in the juxtaposition of the birds and the fans.

I wonder, does he still have the mirror? I stood before it while he stood behind me and . . . Ah well, it was of no great importance. It rarely is of great importance. Though, while I experienced the act, I could only see my face in the mirror. And then my face was not contorted. No, I experienced a momentary contortion which then resolved itself in the Chinese mirror. And I was myself again.

As was he? We never spoke of it. Or of its repetition. For in these matters there is always repetition. I came to rely on it. The reality of the act after so much dreaming was a comfort. He was the first. The other conjunction was not undertaken in a normal fashion. Nor for normal reasons. I understood, of course. They say that to understand all is to forgive all. But forgiveness has its own complicity.

I engaged in those activities before mirrors in private rooms in order perhaps to prove to us both that we were real. And that the actual event took place. After all, we both of us witnessed it in the mirror. I did not engage in these activities through gratitude. Though in fairness it must be admitted that for a time Lord Grantleigh's defence of me was magnificent.

And there was never coercion on his part. The will to join with him was mine. A natural conclusion. Body following mind. He had always been master of my mind, and a dangerous patron of my art.

For years I didn't paint here. During those times I felt

as though the days washed over me. A colour-wash, which was yellow for some reason. Dripping down in a mesmeric pattern into a river on which I seemed to float. I felt I was carried along slowly on a heavy river of paint. My body never seemed to move. Perhaps it couldn't. Perhaps I was trapped in yellow-coloured quick-sand. I never spoke. I washed, endlessly. And I prayed. Years of washing and praying in my heavy yellow river was a peace beyond imagining.

Years went by when I sat lost in the memory of a single day. And of the weeks before it when I painted a bench yellow to commemorate the death of a child. Whose name I can no longer remember. He drowned. I painted a bench, a glorious white-sun yellow. There was a hint of green. The mother laughed so much when I suggested it.

"Yellow?" she cried. "Y-E-L-L-O-W?"

"Yes, yellow."

"Yes, yellow," I said again. I was her tormentor.

And during those yellow-river days I prayed to colour. I prayed to texture. I prayed to pain. But I never, ever, prayed to God. I felt that I had done enough for Him. I absolved myself of any further responsibility. Back and forth I went to my point of stillness. Godless.

THE STILLEST DAY

I must stop this. Memory maddens. Mad memories are breaking my mind.

There is a bell. In case I am *in extremis*. They will give me extreme unction. Pour liquid on me. Non-reflecting liquid? And with this bell I can summon him. Unnecessary. He was summoned long ago. But it has been a long, circumnavigational journey for him. At the centre of which I have stood quietly, waiting and watching as though in a dream, his circling rotation. Which I always knew must end.

THIRTY-EIGHT

"To be summoned by Bethesda Barnet! Is that our fate, Doctor Strauss? Does she summon *me*? I who rule a silent domain and who can instil fear with an inclination of my head. You see, sir, the state to which she has brought this convent. It is not just the paintings. Which of course I have not seen. And, I hasten to add, do not wish to see. Sister Virginia was ill, yes ill, after a second's glance . . . these paintings are an occasion of sin. I go further. Bethesda Barnet is an occasion of sin. She should be avoided. She *must* be avoided. I am full of anger. In itself a sin. Can you see, sir, what is happening to us? Can you *help* us? You have been sent to help us. Is that not right?"

"Sir, surely it is apparent to you the great distress Reverend Mother feels. Your silence, initially understandable, becomes increasingly, increasingly . . ."

"That bell again, Doctor Strauss. Peremptory. Am I

obliged to answer this summons? Very well, let us go then.''

"After you, Reverend Mother. Sir, would you care to follow us?''

"Into what is clearly Bethesda Barnet's kingdom here on earth. That is what has happened, Doctor Strauss. She has carved out for herself her kingdom here on earth. But she has chosen *my* house, which is God's house.''

The sound of the key in the lock.

"I see you have awakened, Sister Annunciata. Though why I continue to call you 'Sister' I do not know.''

"Perhaps out of kindness, Reverend Mother. Or perhaps because in some way you recognise me as your sister. And as your Sister, Reverend Mother, I beg you this once to let me have a mirror.''

"You know that I expressly forbid mirrors in this convent, Sister Annunciata. And in my opinion you have enjoyed too many concessions.''

"Reverend Mother, I know you have a collection of mirrors. They help you when there is uncertainty over death. Death, which as you know, Reverend Mother, and which of course Doctor Strauss knows, is often more elusive than one thinks. Sir . . . Sir . . . How would you establish the moment of death? Would you use mirrors too? Would you, sir? Sir?''

Silence.

Broken by the approaching footsteps of Sister Jacinta.

"Perhaps, Reverend Mother, you could ask her to bring me a mirror. I promise that should you do this for me I will be more . . . compliant."

"Doctor Strauss?"

"Reverend Mother, I think on this occasion, just this one occasion, that you should grant Sister Annunciata's request. I think it may be helpful . . ."

"Very well, Doctor Strauss. I will follow your advice. Sister Jacinta, kindly bring a mirror for Sister Annunciata. Don't look so frightened, Sister Jacinta. Run for the mirror then run to chapel. And pray for her."

"Thank you, Reverend Mother. And thank you, Sister Jacinta, for your prayers. Tell me, sir, have you ever prayed for me?

"What, no prayers either? Very well, sir. I have a number of questions. Perhaps you can answer them, from the dark.

"Tell me, sir, has anyone ever heard from Samuel Keans? All those years. Nothing? I never painted him. He didn't move me in that way. But he was essential to the edifice, to the structure, to the architecture, of my life in the world.

"And tell me, sir, does Alice Thomas still live? Or

Alice Pearson, as she became? Or are there two women named Pearson in the graveyard?

"And what about the child? To whom, though not its mother, I gave the gift of life. Was it an unwanted gift? Did the life last? I rarely think of her. She meant nothing to me. Nothing. The birth was too difficult. I've heard it said that mothers often turn against the child if the birth was hard.

"And now a question, which perhaps no one can, or will ever finally answer. Did I know that she, Mary Pearson, was dead? Did I pass my mirror before her face to see some smoky vision of her breath upon it? Sometimes I answer, no. No, I didn't.

"Did my mother? No, she did not. She made me cut Mary Pearson. It was an unusual cut, though more common in medieval times. But what could we do?

"There are some questions I myself can answer. Did I bleed when I broke the mirror? No. I'm an artist. I protect my hands. These cuts? These scars? They came later. After the moment of action. And yet it's the moment of action which defines us. Not the before, the endless labyrinthine ways through which we arrive at a single point. But the sudden surge of feeling, the physical experience of an intense and present reality which from then on will define past and future. And in that moment the fine points of conscience of a virtuous life are obliterated by the sudden brutal necessity of action."

And ever closer comes Sister Jacinta. Carrying, I hope, a mirror. So light a step can only be hers. She is so small and round. Features and properties of anatomy for which I have no feeling. My landscape is composed of angles, lines, darkness. She enters the room, that small, round, bright creature carrying the small, round mirror from Reverend Mother's collection.

"Thank you, Sister Jacinta. Allow me a minute to establish my identity. Is that why you forbid mirrors, Reverend Mother? So that none of us can confirm our individual identity? So that we can walk down silent corridors, a mass of black to Mass?"

"Few could doubt *your* identity, Sister Annunciata."

"But who can prove it, Reverend Mother? There, now I can put the mirror down. I'm certain I am here. Do you want to look at yourself, sir? To be confirmed? I could, of course, confirm that you're here. I doubt you would believe me.

"So much that we see and hear we don't believe. We don't believe our senses, do we, sir? Why should we? The hand through the wall, pulling us to the other side. It didn't seem natural when it happened. It seemed quite natural when I painted it. But then those two houses leaned so closely together perhaps they melded into each other in a liquefaction of rage and guilt. And so the man's hand came through the wall and laced me tight against it calling, 'Bethesda. Bethesda Barnet, can you hear me? Can you hear me?'

"I'm trembling. As though something is running through my body. Something malign. I cannot stop trembling. I'm trembling from head to foot. No, Doctor Strauss, don't approach me. Forgive me, gentlemen. Forgive me, Reverend Mother. I would like to retire for some moments. May I take the mirror? Thank you, Doctor Strauss. Forgive me, gentlemen. I will return in minutes. I know you'll wait . . .''

THIRTY-NINE

How many lives have fractured to the sound of echoes from behind closed doors? Because we cannot see the listener does not mean he is not there.

And as I lean against the door of my workroom, I gaze at my three paintings. *Croquis. Etude. Ebauche.* Complete in themselves, yet they remain preparations, only preparations for a final painting.

And I listen while Reverend Mother and Doctor Strauss use words in a frantic attempt to find a way, an opening to an exit, for me. And I wait patiently as ever to hear a single sound from the one who sits beside them.

"How did we arrive here, Doctor Strauss? How on earth did we arrive here at this point in our lives? At this point in the life of our convent. We have lost our way. We seem to have *entirely* lost our way."

"Some lives, Reverend Mother, are shot straight from

the bow. Others circumnavigate before they reach their target. My wife, you see, straight from the bow. Towards music. It makes me shudder to imagine the power of the trajectory. Straight to the target. Hours of practice, finger exercises, every single day.''

In extremis, Doctor Strauss always returns to the source of the pain.

''Daily, dactylic discipline. Yes, Reverend Mother. Daily, dactylic discipline. Each finger, every meal. Did you know that? At every meal she exercises her fingers. Between and indeed before courses. I watch them, those ten assemblages of bone and muscle sheathed in skin with their little pearl transparencies a tip, a top, tapping on the table to a rhythm. I can barely touch my food. Sometimes just looking at her fingers, feeling yes, at those moments I actually feel the pattern of the sounds, I feel them in my stomach. No doubt this is why I cannot eat at home . . .''

''Doctor Strauss! Cease this! I must tell you, Doctor, though I've hesitated to say this before, there is something *unnatural* about your obsessive interest . . . yes, I'm afraid it *is* obsessive, in your wife's fingers.''

''Forgive me, Reverend Mother. Forgive me, sir. Sometimes when I'm with Bethesda Barnet I fear that beneath her madness she has a very clear objective. And that she is approaching a target . . .''

"Doctor Strauss, perhaps you're right. Perhaps that's the essence of life. Certain people straight from the bow. Others circumnavigating. As I have. Yes, I see it now. I circumnavigated. And then the terrible question. Is *this* my target? Did I hear God correctly? What a terrible thing. To have misheard God. Perhaps He was calling me in another direction altogether. I sometimes — not at prayers of course — but in my hours of silence, I sometimes think I hear Him speak of other things. Things which surprise me with their wildness. I came to Him late. Always difficult. One is not certain who has hunted whom. Straight from the bow, no questions, no doubts. That is the best way to live . . . Shhh . . . I can hear her returning . . .''

"Straight from the bow, Reverend Mother? Did I just hear you say 'straight from the bow'?''

"You heard the end of my conversation, Sister Annunciata. You seem better. The trembling has stopped.''

"Yes. Solitude soothes me. And you, Doctor Strauss, were you shot straight from the bow?''

"I think not, Sister Annunciata.''

"Perhaps you were, Doctor Strauss, but you have

always been deflected by the vision of your wife's fingers tapping out the unheard music. Poor Doctor Strauss. You believed my pain was eased by your words during the long days of healing wounds. Wounds which are so much quicker to inflict than they are to heal. Of course, for some the infliction of wounds followed by the affliction of healing is a lifetime's endeavour. No? Not for you, sir?

"Answer me, sir. Answer me. Is the infliction of wounds followed by the affliction of healing a lifetime's endeavour? I am guilty. I am not guilty. I acted. I did not act. I thought. I did not think. Action suspended in thought. Thought suspended in action. The sudden, terrible necessity of action. The life of the mind, sir, may drive us to insanity but action, sir, action may often kill . . .

"The trembling again. I thought it had ceased. I must kneel. I need to be on my knees. I must rock myself backwards and forwards. Don't be alarmed, sir. Doctor Strauss knows I do this for hours. It soothes me. I make no sound. In Ireland I've been told they keen. The note is high, unsettling. I've never heard it. Fear not, sir, I'm not uncomfortable. After some time I'll even forget that I'm here. And then I will forget who I am. And in that peace I will sleep. Forgive me, sir. Forgive me. Forgive me . . ."

And whether forgiven or unforgiven, I am left alone. And as the door opens and allows them their longed-for exit, someone is weeping quietly in the corridor.

FORTY

"Sister Jacinta, *stop* weeping. Sister Jacinta, you may think me harsh but I want you to make your way *this minute* to the kitchens to prepare lunch."

"I'm frightened, Reverend Mother, I'm frightened of her. I feel I will meet her in the corridors. I do not want to meet her alone in the corridors."

"Stop this *immediately*, Sister. She is safely locked in her room."

"With her paintings, Reverend Mother? Sister Virginia has told me . . ."

"Told you? *Told* you? How could she tell you? What of your vow of silence? You and I are the only Sisters in this community who have been given special dispensation to speak for these few days. Stop weeping, Sister Jacinta. Leave us now. I will deal with all of this later. Make your way to the kitchens. *Now*."

"Yes. Yes I will. We have been sent salmon, Reverend Mother. It was delivered this morning . . ."

"Salmon? Salmon in winter? Who delivered it? Where did it come from? Did our patron send it? Direct to the kitchen? Why did you not tell me?"

"Forgive me, Reverend Mother, I thought you already knew."

"I did *not* already know, Sister Jacinta! Please don't start to cry again, Sister Jacinta. Now you must leave."

I hear Sister Jacinta, light of foot, running down the corridor.

"I'm really perplexed, Doctor Strauss. Perhaps the salmon was not meant for us . . ."

"Reverend Mother, we have very important matters to discuss. You yourself were angry with me moments ago when I lost my way in an abstraction, a reverie of my wife's . . ."

"Doctor Strauss, I will *not* speak of what we have just heard in that room. I wish to ignore it. I wish to say 'No, I have *not* heard this'. So let us speak of the salmon for a moment. Why did our patron send salmon? And how could our patron send salmon at this time of the year? Are we about to eat a meal intended for others? Is this a mystery? Is this another mystery? I believe I have on many occasions expressed my objection to this fish.

THE STILLEST DAY

The colour of salmon offends in a convent. That peach
and pink membrane, the thickness – when not smoked
. . . It has the colour of human flesh. Human flesh which
we so rarely see. Even our own. I forbid mirrors in the
Sisters' rooms. Contemplation of one's own body is
obscene. I do not wish to gaze upon succulent salmon,
the colour of which always triumphs over Sister Jacinta's
efforts to conceal its obscenity in a green garland.
Perhaps our patron planned a visit and the salmon was
for him."

"Reverend Mother, our patron never comes without
warning."

"True. Though, of course, he has the right to arrive
at any time. Indeed our patron has a worldly power
which seems on occasion greater than that of The
Lord's. Other than in the matter of transubstantiation, of
course. Transubstantiation. Would so many have died
like Cranmer did, had The Lord spoken of fish or meat?
Bread is such an innocent substance. Impossible to
associate it with muscle and bone. Difficult to associate it
with the concept of a body. Would you agree, Doctor
Strauss, that 'This is my body' would not have worked,
if the sacred food had been fish or fowl, and not
bread?"

"What an interesting point, Reverend Mother. Particularly when one considers *Agnus Dei*. Now, Reverend Mother, I must beg you . . ."

"Forgive me, sir. One becomes so aware of every nuance. Perpetual silence makes one so sensitive. Will I return to silence content that I have said *everything* I wanted to say? It may be some time before I can speak for so long again. Oh dear, I'm consumed with guilt. And I have not as yet even consumed my patron's food which was not meant for me."

"Perhaps, Reverend Mother, our patron sent the salmon for our guest."

"Oh, thank you, thank you, Doctor Strauss. Yes, that's it! Doctor Strauss not only heals the body but his words often provide ointment for my soul. When my soul is fearful."

"It is a doctor's duty, Reverend Mother. For a fearful soul or mind will eventually trouble the body."

"You are so wise, Doctor Strauss. What does our guest think?"

"Will nothing break your silence, sir? Reverend Mother and I are desperate. We make frantic efforts to fill each moment with conversation in order to ameliorate what might be interpreted as your sullen silence."

"You rise, sir, to leave us? Will you not join us for

lunch? Doctor Strauss, why is our guest leaving us? So suddenly. Does he know what he *must* do? Doctor Strauss, have we made ourselves clear? Did he hear the lines that mattered? It's so hard in all we hear to know the lines that matter. Before you leave, sir . . ."

"Desist, Reverend Mother. I think our guest has heard the lines that matter. I think our guest is a good and faithful servant who has come about his master's business."

FORTY-ONE

The notes tell us that the guest broke his silence on the following day, Tuesday, both during the morning and also late in the afternoon.

Certain sounds echoed down the corridors. Unrecognisable.

One sister believed she heard laughter. But there is no proof. And if laughter was heard what did it denote?

That night, before the guest left the room of Bethesda Barnet, he requested of Sister Jacinta and of Reverend Mother, who had accompanied her when she responded to the ringing of the bell, the following items. Linen, blankets, paper and much twine.

Later he was seen to leave the room of Bethesda Barnet carrying what the witness believed were three paintings. They were meticulously wrapped and one must infer from the thickness of the wrapping that underneath the paper were layers of protective linen.

The guest stated to Sister Jacinta and to Reverend Mother

THE STILLEST DAY

that he would see Bethesda Barnet alone at dawn the following morning. He gave further orders that he did not wish to be disturbed during the night.

As Doctor Strauss had been called urgently to his wife's bedside by a frantic messenger claiming that she had mutilated her hands, this record of Tuesday's events is corroborated only by Sister Jacinta and Reverend Mother, Sister Superior of the Order of the Immaculate Conception on the island of S.

FORTY-TWO

On this, another Wednesday before Ash Wednesday a stranger on the shore would discern only a boat and perhaps the outline of two bodies. Mine and yours. A stranger might even wave across the waves to us, believing distance protected him. Not knowing that accident can make us witness, even from afar. For if caught, though it be at the very edge of the painting, we remain forever caught.

Shall I whisper to you as we sit together on this short journey from island to mainland? As the cypress trees, circumferential guardians of my island life, slip from view, their reflection lost in white fog, shall I whisper? Now that I am no longer hidden by trees or stones and now that the sanctuary of ritual and routine has been torn down and crumbles around me, shall I whisper to you the words which drift in a dawn delirium round and round in my mind? Unpainted questions, as yet unasked.

THE STILLEST DAY

Who was it on that day who bent and carefully gathered up blood-stained splinters of mirror, those lethal shards which lay about Mary Pearson's body? Since I know the answer and have always known it, I could frame other, darker questions. Where did you hide the fragments of mirrored you? Are they buried somewhere, their luminescence dulled by the earth, or are they in a secret place you visit to catch a reflection of reflection?

Why did you remain silent in the room where judge and jury, Lord Grantleigh, the Bishop and the doctor, were seated? For had you spoken, another colour would have seeped insidiously into the minds of those three men. Men who had discreetly shrouded in silence the hours they had not witnessed in order to hand to a village and its children a gift of eternal assurance. Had you let fall into that silence certain words, those men might more diligently have searched in the debris of that day. For your words would have altered the very nature of the action and, though innocent, perhaps have proved me guilty. And for that silence you have long punished yourself. And me. You saved me from retribution for a sin I had not committed. But we are often more harshly punished for the sins we did not commit than for those we did.

And now onto this morning fog, I could paint fragile

lines of yearning, silvery with doubt. Is silver the colour of doubt? What shapes its lines, these gossamer hieroglyphics which dance together into a configuration of "Did you come for me? Or did he send you for the paintings?"

And the silhouetted letters shiver in the wind and are lost. I make no effort to retrieve them. Instead, I wonder do you have a recollection of yourself? Do you discern the outline of yourself in the paintings? And in tracing what you believe to be a recognisable line, do you also trace the shape of fear? The fear of being trapped forever in a painting?

And I dream of how you wrapped the paintings carefully, slowly, in layers of linen beneath layers of blankets beneath layers of paper. And shreds of other thoughts assemble into a mosaic of an insubstantial future, in which I wonder, who will cut through all this? Through this forest of paper, wool and linen? And will he recognise what he has found? I once cut. And in a trance-like violence I searched. And I found life. Life, which like death, is indisputable.

There are paintings which we dream and then long to make substantial. Now I will paint a dream. The body, shivering beneath my habit which I now lay down and from which I break free, will be my canvas. Naked, the wasteland of my body stands for a second before you. It is a sad offering, pallid and pathetic, crying out for colour, rich and deep.

Now I touch the head land, a waste of old and heavy hair which has long lain hidden by its dark veil. This hair, uncut, another breaking of the rules, had been laid out only at night on a white, endlessly-mended, cotton pillow case in the hope that in the moon's reflection it might be strung out tight by an unseen hand. Which would play upon it the longed-for scales of pain?

It is too late a disrobing. You barely glance at me. You seem not to note that my throat is rippled with a filigree of tiny scratches such as a bird's claw might leave. Tiny scratches such as Ingres made on his pupils' paintings for correction. And now the shawl of fog slips briefly from my breasts and their blind eyes gaze back at you. There is a sudden involuntary widening of your pupils before you look away.

Your sigh, almost a shudder, slips away and then dips like the oars into silence. You have come a long journey and know well for what you wait. This lake is deep and its deepest point is here. And even as we draw closer to the shore the watcher sees little and therefore remains innocent of all.

My body has adjusted to the cold and no longer

shivers. And though I am so close to you, you do not look at me. You are insensible to this assembly of named parts, the canvas on which I will create a final painting. *Croquis. Etude. Ebauche;* three stages in its preparation lie beside you in the boat. I know that you will guard them well.

Now a last painting will be my gift to you to assuage long hunger and grief. Through the years I have felt your hunger. It devoured me, as it devoured you. For we all need someone else to bleed. I know now that nothing less will do. And when I have finished my painting and have given you my gift I know that you will weep and smile and, having wept, and smiled, will return to your life, your mainland life.

And I call out to you at last. And at last you bend towards me, still beautiful, still silver-white in all this whiteness. And I smile at you and ask,

"Boatman . . . will you guide me through the landscape of a dream to the still moment of another reality, an elsewhere?"

The oars continue their measured movement and no sound beats out to accompany them. Such long, silent patience must be rewarded. I commence my work.

"This is for you. This painting, which no other man will ever see. And no man ever has, nor ever will have, such a gift bestowed upon him. It comes with total absolution.

"So sit and watch now as I break another painted mirror. Onto which you have been reflected again. Reverend Mother will in time come to regret her reluctant concession. I cut here. Can you see? Can you see the laceration? Watch the colour come and go. Pure red. Unrivalled by the artist. Watch it, drop by drop, fall slowly, soundlessly on obdurate wood."

Now you watch. And you wait. And though I speak softly you do not again bend towards me. And I know that you never will.

This painting needs a deeper colour. With this mirrored image of your hand I draw more blood to my white forehead. I can feel the line is good. Do you admire its perfection? Mark the contrast, the vibrancy of the drenched red on the white forehead. Note the circular drops now, here, on my cheek. The slight discolouration of the tongue as it darts to drink or at least receive some of this last libation. As the tongues of the Sisters greedily receive the body and blood so generously meted out to them.

"I have chosen for you a palette of decadent red. With it I will now paint a crucifix on my breast. So fast. The painter is in a trance. Is the watcher entranced? Still no word from you? Watch me while I draw a rope of tiny ruby indentations to mark a waist unmarked before. Repetition demeans the artist so this cut is different. It is not as I cut her. Do you remember? Do you remember the cut? It was long and deep. Cavernous. From which I pulled the child.

"Who had my courage? Who has ever had my courage? Will you remember these questions, years from now? And if you remember, will you answer them years from now?"

Do you, I wonder, approve my handiwork? Do you approve your handiwork? My weapon bears the outline of your hand upon it. You're growing paler. But wait, I will grow whiter still than you. Whiteness beyond whiteness. Purity beyond purity. You cannot move. Or you will not move. This does not shock me. Why should you strive to prevent what you have long dreamed of? How we should give thanks for our unpunished dreams.

I need a final sustenance. First I'll swallow tiny slivers. Then quickly cut the throat along a necklace of careful stitches.

"Are you thirsty? Do you want to drink? Quick, quick. A rain-washed face . . . rain-washed . . . and silver-white . . ."

THE STILLEST DAY

Now I slip away into silence and the water. And as I drift away from you all the colour of my painting gathers into a single rivulet of red flowing back to you, as I grow whiter and whiter and rise and fall, whiter and whiter in cold, silver-reflecting water.

I taught children once. All the old essential lies. Life. I float away from you. At last I'm borne away. From life. Life which is perhaps best lived as a dream.

Thomas Argyll, Esq.
Christie, Manson & Woods,
8 King Street,
St James's
London

Dear Thomas,

The answer is yes. I will sell the paintings. Frankly, I was unaware until your letter and subsequent visit that anyone knew of their existence.

I thought once that I would never part with them. They cost me dear in more ways than I can tell you. But that was long ago . . . and besides . . .

I now wish to be rid of them. My son, poor George, never had any interest in art. Perhaps if he'd lived . . . So many sons have died in this war. There is so much that we will never know.

On my death Grantleigh Manor and all its contents will pass to Alexander, my brother's son. The paintings are not a happy bequest. It is best if they take their leave of my family entirely.

Should your unnamed buyer decide not to proceed, let us attempt to dispose of the paintings at the next appropriate sale.

In that case provenance should remain anonymous. The paintings should be referred to as "Property of a Gentleman". Which I suppose I still am, Thomas.

Yours,

Grantleigh